Edgar Barclay

Mountain Life in Algeria

Edgar Barclay

Mountain Life in Algeria

ISBN/EAN: 9783337288006

Printed in Europe, USA, Canada, Australia, Japan

Cover: Foto ©Andreas Hilbeck / pixelio.de

More available books at **www.hansebooks.com**

ALGERIA

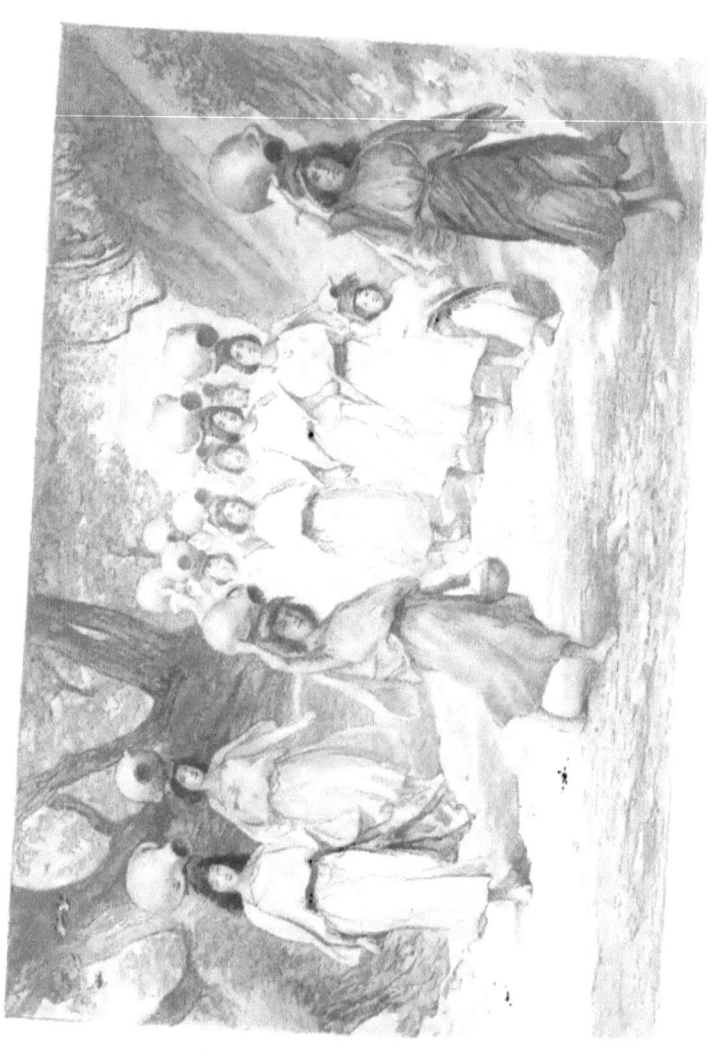

MOUNTAIN LIFE IN ALGERIA

BY

EDGAR BARCLAY

WITH ILLUSTRATIONS BY THE AUTHOR

LONDON
KEGAN PAUL, TRENCH, & CO., 1 PATERNOSTER SQUARE
1882

INTRODUCTION.

FROM the city of Algiers, looking eastwards across the bay, is seen a snow-covered mass towering above lower ranges of mountains. It is to the country lying immediately beneath those snow-clad peaks, inhabited by a people of entirely different race and speech to the Arabs, and known as Kabyles, that the following pages relate. Though Algiers has many English visitors, this district remains little known; the reason perhaps being the want of those accommodations that tourists look for.

A day spent at Fort National, which is at the threshold of the region I refer to, is usually considered ample, and exhausts their interest. But any one making a more prolonged stay in a country, is apt to look upon it in a different light to the passing traveller; and I may be pardoned for having taken up the pen, if I should succeed in inspiring the reader with some of the interest that I feel for this district and its native inhabitants.

In former days, when the Kabyles were self-governing, immemorial custom, religion, and tribal laws, rigidly enforced hospitality. Special funds were put aside by the Jemãa, or village Com-

mune, for the entertainment of travellers ; it held itself responsible
for the safety of the stranger and for that of his luggage, and each
householder was in his turn called upon to play the part of host.

At present, under French rule, it is obligatory for the Amine,
or headman, to entertain a stranger for one night.   If it were not
for this law, it is clear that, as there are no inns, a European
journeying through the country might, by the caprice of the natives,
be forced to pass the night without shelter on the mountain side.

The Amine refuses the money offered him in requital, but
some one can always be found to accept a suitable payment.

The house where the traveller may be entertained, will probably
be constructed in somewhat the following fashion.

A series of rooms is built round an open courtyard, which has
a single entrance, and within which cattle, sheep, and goats are
driven for protection at night.   The building is of blocks of stone
roughly plastered together, and whitewashed over.   The beams
and rafters of the roof are apparent, and upon them is spread a
thick layer of canes, the crannies between being filled up with
earth ; above is a covering of tiles, and on these again heavy
stones help by their weight to keep the whole in its place.   The
eaves are broad, and sometimes project so far over the courtyard
that they are supported by wooden columns, and thus form a rude
corridor, which affords shelter for the beasts from the weather.

Is not such a courtyard the model of the rude ancestor of such
refined examples as are to be seen at Pompeii, where the open

enclosure for the protection of animals has grown into a fountain-refreshed garden, and the rustic corridor into one decorated with elegant encaustic paintings ?

In some parts of the country, large flattened slabs of cork are substituted for tiles, and are laid overlapping in the manner of slates ; a layer of earth is beaten down on the top, which soon becomes overgrown with moss and weeds. These roofs are much flatter than the tiled ones, being just sufficiently inclined to throw off water when it rains heavily ; they thus form terraces useful for various purposes, such as drying fruit. The rooms are lighted chiefly from their doorways, which lead from the court-yard, but in the outer walls are a few windows just large enough to permit a person's head being protruded. Rooms are set apart for the women and children of the household, and on one side of the courtyard is the guest chamber. On entering this, the stranger is struck by finding it resemble a barn, rather than an ordinary room at an inn. The roof is sup-ported by columns and beams, made from the roughly trimmed trunks of trees, and the floor is of beaten plaster. At one end of the room is a wall about five feet in height, supporting a broad platform or stage, on which are placed gigantic earthenware jars, square in plan, and five or six feet in height. These contain a provision of dried figs and grain, which is thus secured from damp and the attacks of rats. The platform is the roof of a stable for the accommodation of mules and cows. The room has only one door, which serves also as a passage to this stable. The beasts entering, turn, and are driven down an inclined plane, which opens between the outer wall of the building and the wall supporting the platform, and find themselves in their stalls. The floor of the stable is three or four feet lower than where the guest reclines, who is startled at seeing the heads of the beasts appear at large square openings, on a level with, and facing him.

This singular arrangement has at any rate the merit of allowing the traveller to observe whether his animals are properly cared for, since literally they sup at the sideboard.

Thoughts also are likely to arise concerning the Nativity, and how the infant Saviour was laid in his swaddling-clothes in a manger ; for here is an example, that the most natural course to adopt, supposing that there should be an extra number of guests, would be to enter the stable under the same roof.

In one corner is a small hole made in the floor, where live embers are placed if the weather be cold, the smoke finding its exit as best it can through a hole above. Rugs are spread on the floor, and in due time the evening meal is brought, which will include a Kouskous, the characteristic dish of the country, answering to the macaroni of Southern Italy.

The Amine and some of his friends, sit by while the guest eats; but they do not partake themselves, their *rôle* is, to enliven the stranger with their conversation, to serve him, and to encourage him to eat as much as he can. When he has finished they retire, leaving a guardian who sleeps just within the threshold. The traveller rolls himself up in his wraps, and disposes himself to sleep upon the floor. Even if tired, he is fortunate if he wake refreshed in the morning, for sometimes there may be other animals besides cows and mules—rats in the roof or about the bins, not to mention fleas, the dogs of the house bark, and jackals howl outside.

Such being a picture of the native accommodation, it is evident that a European proposing to remain in the country, away from French settlements, must travel with a tent. The opportunity to do so, was offered me by Colonel Playfair, Her Majesty's Consul-General at Algiers, who most kindly placed his fine tent at my disposal ; and I take this occasion to again thank him for the shelter under which I spent so many pleasant days and peaceful nights.

I have been asked, ' What do you find attractive in this semi-barbarous Kabylia ?' Before relating my story, it will not be out of place to mention a few facts relating to the country, which in my estimation render it interesting for an artist.

Firstly, the landscape combines great beauty with an imposing grandeur. There is a luxuriance of vegetation which more than rivals that of Southern Italy ; and the glorious mountain masses, with their scarped precipices, cannot be easily matched for their form and colour.

The land is highly cultivated, and of a happy and cheerful aspect.

It is thickly populated, and the out-of-door life of the people, both as regards their agricultural and pastoral occupations, is picturesque. Not that these are strange in their character, on the contrary, they have the charm of being simple world-wide performances, common to all time.

The women, although Mohammedans, expose their faces with the same freedom as Europeans.

The dress of the men consists of a tunic and burnous.

The artistic merit of this loose and extremely simple dress, is not in the actual clothes, but in the manner of wearing them, which is varied. From the arrangements of folds into which these garments fall being ever changing, the artistic sense of the observer is always kept alive. A man thus simply dressed, may by some chance movement fling his cloak about his person, so that its masses and folds assume a dignity and interest worthy of permanence in sculpture. Such harmonies unfold themselves suddenly, and are fleeting, but they are an incentive to endeavour to record them.

I believe this is the only corner of the world, where the dress of the women is still the same as the Greek dress of antiquity. Though the Romans dominated North Africa, there is no reason to suppose that it was introduced by them ; because, in a certain condition of society, it is the dress which common sense dictates.

Gestures can be studied when the people are excited, but only then. I should describe the ordinary manners of the Kabyles as gentle and calm; but at times, when their passions are aroused, they are as vehement as the storms that break the serenity of their climate. They are not as a rule a fussy gesticulating people; on the contrary, at the entrance to a village, a rustic row can always be found chatting peacefully, and sitting very still. Nor is it only the old who thus indulge in sunning themselves, though they can be seen there also, who

> Wise through time and narrative with age
> In summer days like grasshoppers rejoice,
> A bloodless race that send a feeble voice.

With us, it is by all classes felt that it is wise for a man to keep his head as cool as he can, but the Kabyles, in the ordinary way so quiet and gentle in demeanour, are an impulsive people, careless of self-control, and a mere trifle is sufficient to enflame them. They freely give reins to their feelings, untrammelled by considerations which beset more civilised men; and when passions have unrestrained play, gestures, which are the pantomime of passion, are born.

Owing to their having remained uninfluenced by strangers, there is a remarkable harmony between their manners and customs, and the country they inhabit; and on account of the simplicity of life, the reason for things being constructed and arranged as they are is generally traceable, and this gives an agreeable impression. The villages, for instance, seem to grow naturally out of the mountains, and the dress of the people accords exactly with their con-

ditions of life. Their artificial surroundings are very meagre, hard,
unalluring and rude ; but at any rate it is satisfactory to find them
free from the qualities of foolishness and insincerity ; for when men
seek simply to satisfy their wants, they are sure to act sensibly, and,
according to their ability, adapt means to ends in the most direct
manner possible. There is no place for trick and sham ; moreover, when they decorate anything, they follow a simple tradition,
but keep their personal feeling and invention alive, and thus
they avoid the two sins of vulgarity and insipidity. All work so
done, however rude it may be, is respectable and interesting.

This sense of harmony is felt all the more strongly by glancing
for a moment at one of the new French settlements on the borders
of the same country, where its absence is conspicuous ; it is at
once obvious, that such a village belongs to a complicated system
of society.

The Kabyle village is rude and simple, the French is mean
without being simple. It is built on the dusty high road, which
can be seen winding in a serpentine line like a white thread,
through the feverish plains. The road is traced in accordance with
military and strategic reasons, and it will be found that there is
little sign of traffic : a broad mule-track well trodden down, runs
near, following a straighter line though more uneven gradients.
This gives the road the appearance of being a sham. The village
consists of a collection of hideous little houses sprinkled about
in the plain, without shade from the pitiless sun, mean oblong

boxes, quite unlike the model of a *colon's* house that was to be seen
in the gardens of the Trocadero at Paris in 1878, which showed a
beautiful power of idealising. A government order has fixed the
colony in its place, which so far as can be seen, might as well have
been chosen at any other point. An ugly little church has been
just completed, which the inhabitants do not appear either to
respect or to want. All the wood used in the construction of
the buildings has been brought from over the seas, from Norway,
though the sides of the hills are covered with trees. The most
frequented place of meeting is the dram-shop, where the heralds
of civilisation congregate to tipple absinthe. Speak to the
colonists, you will find that they abuse their homes and their
circumstances ; they one and all wish that they were somewhere
else, perhaps the only point on which the natives are ready to
agree with them. ' Peut-être—oui, peut-être, le pays est joli, mais
vu du loin,' is the nearest approach to praise that I have been able
to extract from a colonist in such a village.

In England men adapt their lives to the requirements and the
accumulated conveniences of civilisation ; but in a primitive
society, there is a forced accordance between man and surrounding nature, which imposes its conditions upon life.

In Kabylia this agreement is visible in every particular and
detail of life. Those bronzed and furrowed features, those sinewy
limbs, do they not attest struggle and toil with nature ? Watch
those girls as they trip down the mountain path ; at every step

their movements are governed by the accidents of the ground.
What a path it is! Fit emblem of half-civilised institutions.
Year after year, year after year, it receives the impress of many
feet, yet all the rude asperities of nature remain.

Kabylia has I think another interest, purely fanciful. On
seeing the villages with tiled roofs set on the tops of the mountains,
surrounded by fig-trees ; and corn ripening among the fine olives ;
one is irresistibly reminded of Italy. But here, though the people
are of a different race and religion, they have retained the habits
of a very primitive age ; and in this corner of the world, more
than anywhere in Europe, observation of the manners of to-day,
will picture the rural life of classic times.

Upon observing a phase of life so different from the world one
is accustomed to, it is agreeable to discover that in odd unexpected
ways, it connects itself in the mind, with a past whose beauty
remains recorded for our enjoyment.

Added to these points of interest that Kabylia offers to the
artist, there is the advantage that the climate is healthy and
invigorating.

I first visited this country in the early spring of the year 1873,
when I spent several weeks there. I revisited it in the year 1877,
when I remained over a month among the mountains, living part
of the time with Italians at an isolated farmhouse, and part of the
time with the Missionary Fathers. In the beginning of 1880, I
again returned and stayed a month at Fort National, and in April

started on the expedition recorded in this narrative. On this last occasion I kept a diary. On my return home, I found that my notes were too concise to conjure up scenes to others ; nevertheless they elicited so many enquiries, that I resolved to expand them in my leisure hours. The following is the result. In the hope that it may interest a wider circle than my personal friends, I with diffidence submit it to public criticism.

LIST OF ILLUSTRATIONS

DRAWN BY THE AUTHOR.

———◆———

PHOTO ENGRAVINGS.

WOOD ENGRAVINGS.

> As man conversing man,
> Met at an oak.
>
> POPE'S *Iliad*, Book xxii.

> Like some fair olive, by my careful hand
> He grew, he flourish'd, and adorn'd the land.
>
> POPE'S *Iliad*, Book xviii.

> The season now for calm, familiar talk,
> Like youths and maidens in an evening walk.
> POPE'S *Iliad*, Book xxii.

> And naked sow the land,
> For lazy winter numbs the lab'ring hand.
> DRYDEN'S *Virgil*, Georgic i.

> 'Tis more by art than force of numerous strokes,
> The dexterous woodman shapes the stubborn oaks.
> POPE'S *Iliad*, Book xxiii.

> As when ashore an infant stands,
> And draws imagin'd houses in the sands.
> POPE'S *Iliad*, Book xv.

HEADINGS TO CHAPTERS.

MEN MET AT AN OAK.

As man conversing man,
Met at an oak

Pope's *Iliad.* Book xxii.

MOUNTAIN LIFE IN ALGERIA.

CHAPTER I.

EFORE leaving Algiers, my friend Muir-
head and I engaged a Frenchman as a
servant, who undertook, in accompanying
us, to guard the tent during our absence,
and to cook.

This matter being arranged, he went
with us on a shopping expedition, when
we purchased the necessary kitchen utensils, and got them packed
in a conveniently shaped box. We filled our empty tins with
provisions, and supplied ourselves with a few medicines, a pre-
cautionary measure that happily proved superfluous.

Muirhead bought an excellent folding camp-bed at Attaracks',
the army purveyors. For myself, I took an Indian bullock-trunk,
containing clothes, books, and a store of photographic gelatine
plates ; and a box with painting materials and a camera. Folding

irons by uniting these two packages formed a bedstead, upon which a cork mattress could be spread. A carpenter made for me a flat case to hold canvases, which served also as an easel, having pieces of wood so arranged on one side that they could be slipped down to form leg supports. This proved convenient; it was strong, so simple that it could not get out of order, and it could be adjusted so as to stand firm however uneven the ground.

Our preparations completed, we took places in the diligence leaving for Tizi-Ouzou, a French settlement on the borders of Kabylia. We started April 6, 1880.

The diligence left at the inconvenient hour of eight o'clock in the evening, and arrived at its destination at eight the following morning; we had a very uncomfortable, sleepless ride, and at Tizi-Ouzou only remained long enough to breakfast, after which we took the omnibus for Fort National.

The fort is built in a commanding position, at the top of a mountain 3,153 feet in height. The road at first passes through a plain, crosses the river Sebaou, which is not bridged and is liable to freshets after rain, when it becomes impassable.

The omnibus, on account of the snapping of one of the springs, made unusually slow progress as it toiled along the zigzag road leading up to the Fort. We consequently got out and walked most of the way, taking short cuts, and greatly enjoying the deliciously fresh air and fine scenery, and arrived at our destination between one and two o'clock, when, having refreshed ourselves, we took a turn outside the ramparts for the sake of the superb view from this point. There was a grand tumble of mountains, range beyond range; but what riveted our attention chiefly were the great peaks and rocky masses of the Jurjura to the south.

As I already knew something of the country, and Muirhead saw it for the first time, he said, 'And what do you propose doing?' I accordingly suggested that we should go in the direction of the high mountains, where we should be most likely to find points of interest. There were two roads in front of us, both leading to places suitable for camping. The first was on the crest of a mountain range, studded with many villages that lay between us and the peaks of the Jurjura, the seat of the Beni Ienni, one of the best-known tribes in the country, where native jewellery and cutlery is chiefly manufactured. The second was the home of the Aïth Ménguellath; their mountain was not actually visible, being hidden by the spurs of the one on which we were standing; it was farther off, but more easy of access than the Beni Ienni, being skirted by the French road to Akbou, the only one leading out of the country in the direction of Constantine, Kabylia being otherwise an 'impasse.' The latter tribe have in their midst a school under the direction of three missionary Fathers, and the former a school superintended by three Jesuit Fathers. We anticipated that the presence of the good Pères would be of service to us, considering our ignorance of the language.

At our feet, between us and the Beni Ienni, was a deep gulf. The Kabyle road before us, rough and steep, led down into it, apparently ending in the blue distance in a fine example of the perpendicular; the other wound round to the left at a high level. After a little talk over the matter, we decided to follow the civilised line as the easier, and to start for the Aïth Ménguellath the following morning, provided that we could find mules. We soon found there was no difficulty on this point, and five were promised to be ready at an early hour. When several mules are engaged, each belonging to a different owner, a considerable amount of excited talk and gesticulation has to be got through before the traveller sees his luggage finally packed and ready to start, for each mule-owner naturally does his best to get the heavy pieces put on his neighbour's mule and the light pieces on his own. In the midst of all this dispute and fuss, the mules stand patiently, but they have a trick of striking out their legs, as if it were only just as much as they could do to support their burdens ; more luggage is heaped on their backs, their expression of countenance grows more wistful and dejected ; but when everything is adjusted they prick up their ears and start jauntily. We had three beasts, heavily laden, and two riding-mules. It was a glorious, perfect morning ; the sun warm, the air brisk ; and the great range of lofty mountains tipped with snow looked most sublime. We caught the country in the very act of bedecking itself with its spring mantle, for the mountain slopes were covered with the bright fresh green of the young corn, and the ash-trees in abundance were just opening their delicate leaves.

On the way we passed one or two small villages, and some charming wooded gullies with falling streams. At such a spot was a scene that caught my fancy. A party of girls had placed some clothes on smooth rocks, in the run of the brook, and, barefooted, were merrily dancing upon them ; others were flopping about a crimson dress, previous to wringing it, while more clothes lay drying in the sun on the grassy slope. Above them, offering shade for a noontide repast, rose an elegant ash, with a great vine mazily tangled up with and depending from its branches. The eastern end of the mountain was not so verdant as the country we had already passed, the ground being naturally more barren ; but no square foot of land capable of cultivation had been neglected, and it was matter of wonder to see corn growing on slopes so steep that no one could stand on them without some caution lest he should roll to the bottom of the ravine ; as, moreover, it was by no means obvious where the bottom might be, and pretty evident that anyone rolling down would have no sound bone left in his body by the time he reached it, one could not but admire the plucky industry of the Kabyles.

The house of the Missionary Fathers at length appeared in the distance on a well-wooded ridge, the higher points of which were crowned by three or four large villages.

The road now became unfit for carriages, and dwindled to a mule-path, winding in an irregular fashion. We passed one especially picturesque place, crowned by the white tower of a mosque, with a fine group of evergreen oaks shading the rocky corner of a cemetery. As we approached the Aïth Ménguellath, and made the final ascent to the Mission House, the path was shaded by avenues of ash-trees.

On knocking at the door of the school-house, we found only one of the Fathers at home ; he received us very politely, and refreshed us with excellent wine, made on the lands of the fraternity at the Maison Carrée, a few miles from Algiers, where is their mother establishment. Their Superior is the Bishop of Algiers.

Any young man desirous of entering the society commences with a course of study in Arabic, at their house at the Maison Carrée. They have four other schools in Kabylia, besides this in the Aïth Ménguellath, which is the latest founded, and the Jesuits have two establishments.

On the road, we had seen no level piece of ground suitable for camping. In answer to our inquiries, the Father thought that nowhere in the neighbourhood could be found a better place than beside a small cemetery just beneath the school-house, where our animals had that moment halted; we therefore lost no time in unlading the mules, and dismissing our attendant Kabyles. We had never before pitched the tent, which was a large and fine one, unusual in its arrangements, and it took us some time to put it up; we were much embarrassed by tombstones, these encroached so near that it was next to impossible to peg down the tent. However, when once it was up, with the lining, and our camp-beds and luggage disposed within, it looked very comfortable. We determined that while we remained dwellers beside tombs, however much the ghosts of the departed might be perturbed at the unwonted presence of the unfaithful, our peace should remain secure.

A few men had collected to watch our proceedings, and boys from the school gathered round. They were a nice-looking set of lads, bright and gentle-mannered, and we were glad to find that they possessed a stock of French, slender though it was. The fire flickered up, in preparation for our evening meal, the school-lads in their white burnouses stood round, whilst through the trees the Jurjura peaks grew dim in the fading light.

Our man, Domenique, came from the Pyrenees on the Spanish

frontier; he called himself a Frenchman, but he did not look
like one, nor had he the lively French manners. He was spare,
of about forty, with black straight hair and moustache, black eyes,
under-cut mouth, with marked lines about the jaw. From the
beginning, Muirhead declared him to be a man with a temper,
which proved to be too true; time also proved him to be a man of
a bilious temperament, utterly incapable of understanding a joke.
'He is quite the Spanish type,' said Muirhead. I know not, but
if Spaniards are apt to resemble him, I hope I may never travel
in their country.

We both of us marvelled greatly at the wonderfully meagre
preparation he had made for his personal comfort. He carried
with him nothing but a striped cloth, and a very thin green cardboard box, done up with string. To the last, the contents of this
package were a mystery to us, but we believe that it contained a
shirt-front, and one or two collars.

Such unpreparedness, such despising of all worldly comfort,
should, we thought, be surely viewed from above by the saints
with approving smiles, and Saint Joseph especially should have
regarded with favour this extreme scantiness of scrip, which,
judging from pictures, should have reminded him of his own
'Flight into Egypt.'

Friday, April 9, 1880.—We paid an early call at the school-
house, and saw the three Fathers. I found the Superior, Père
Gerboin, to be a friend. Two years previously, I had spent a week
at his house; he was then conducting a school in the tribe of the
Zouardia, and I was indebted to his hospitality for the opportunity
of seeing something of the tribes away from French settlements.

He is a most excellent, kindly man, devoted to his calling. One would take him rather for an Italian than a Frenchman; short but strongly built, he has a handsome head, with a deep brow, and a flowing black beard, his bronzed features are set off by his white dress, which is something between that of a Carmelite friar and a Kabyle burnous.

The second, Père Voisin by name, whom I had not met, is almost a giant, over six feet in height, and fair; a true Norman, from Calvados, a jolly, lively fellow, his face a picture of good nature, and he speaks Kabyle with the ease of a native.

Père Gerboin teaches the elder boys; Père Voisin takes in hand a class of quite little fellows. About thirty scholars attend regularly, but the numbers are increasing.

The third, Père Mousallier, we had spoken to on our arrival; he is called by the natives Père Baba. He was busy making up and distributing medicines, for he said there was much disease and sickness about—not to be wondered at, considering the lack of doctors, and the hard life led by many of the people. He spends a good deal of his time in gardening, but does not take part in the teaching.

Our visit was but short, for we started on a walk of exploration, first directing our steps towards the highest point, at the back of the school-house, where there are two villages, separated by a small open piece of flat land. These are named Ouarzin and Taourirt en Taïdith, meaning the Ogre, and the Mount of the Dog. They are of the usual quaint character, narrow alleys, running irregularly up and down, innocent of paving, though rich in stones; in wet weather almost impassably muddy. The stone walls of the houses, on either side of these alleys, are only pierced here and there, with the smallest of windows, and the entrances. The wooden doors are often ornamented with rough notchings and carvings. In walking through these villages, attention is chiefly occupied in looking out for dogs, which are apt to come dashing out of the houses, barking in a most vicious manner, looking very much as if they would relish a piece out of one's leg. Taourirt boasts of a Jamâ or Mosque. Its tower crowns the highest point of the mountain, and forms an effective feature in the landscape, though it is a modest structure both in size and style; moreover, the building is greatly out of repair and falling to pieces, being little used, for the Kabyles are not a mosque-going people; in this, as in other respects, their character presents a strong contrast to that of the bigoted Arabs.

I once asked a Kabyle why their mosques were abandoned. He replied that, before they were conquered by the French, they used to attend them very regularly, and that if Allah had cared about their conduct, and paid attention to it, He would not have allowed them to receive the kicks and cuffs of a too hard fate, such as they had been subject to ever since. This man was clearly of a practical bent of mind, and his God was the God of Battles. This is a proof of ancient and respectable theological views, that have the merit of being intelligible; their scientific notions seem to be equally primitive.

On one occasion a group of Kabyles was standing round, when I abruptly left off working, and began gathering my painting traps together, for, said I, 'I see the wind is blowing the clouds in this direction, it will rain.' 'The wind does not push the clouds,' said one, 'you can see them moving in different directions at the same time.' 'But surely,' said I, 'you can perceive any day that it is the wind that moves them.' 'Does the wind move the sun?' said he. 'No, of course it doesn't.' 'God said to the sun, Move always in one direction, and to the clouds He said, Move about as you please.' 'Is that not so?' said he, appealing to his companions. They nodded gravely, and clicked assent without speaking. This clicking with the tongue, the same peculiar noise that a coachman makes to urge his horse, is a habit with the Kabyles; it seems to be a sign of assent. For instance, when painting, some men would come to see what I was about. One would say, 'See, he paints the cows!'—click! would go all the others, like so many pistols being cocked. 'See, he paints the houses also!'—click! they went, all round again, but no report followed—a feeble style of criticism.[1]

I have often noticed that in asking some simple question concerning the weather—for instance, whether it was likely to turn fine, or be wet—they seem to consider it presumptuous to hazard an opinion on such a subject, that we should leave such matters alone, and not think about them, they being no concern of ours, but

---

[1] I am not aware whether anyone has previously remarked that the Kabyles click. In a paper published by the Society of Arts, March 4, 1881, on the Languages of Africa, by Robert N. Cust, I was amused to learn that clicking is common to many languages. Speaking of the Hottentots, Mr. Cust says: 'The great feature of the language is the existence of four clicks, formed by a different position of the tongue; the dental click is almost identical with the sound of indignation, not unfrequently uttered by Europeans; the lateral click is the sound with which horses are stimulated to action; the guttural click is not unlike the popping of a champagne cork; and the palatal click is compared to the cracking of a whip.' He says that the Bushman, in addition to the four clicks of the Hottentot language, has a fifth, sixth, and sometimes a seventh and eighth. According to Bleek and Lepsius, two authorities, Hottentot is, curiously, entirely distinct from other languages spoken by black races, and is connected with the Hamitic languages of white races of North Africa.

God's. Their manner implies that we should bear ourselves with a composed spirit, above a petty, fretful, unmanly prying into the works of the Lord. I have immediately dropped my eyes from the clouds to the earth, feeling quite abashed and inclined to say, ' Bless my soul! why, so it is, now you mention it, I will not meddle with the subject any more, and never, oh, never look at telegrams in the " Times " concerning the wind, whence it cometh or whither it goeth.'

Each village has usually three or four outlets, where there are covered resting-places called Jamâs. These, like the houses, are of rough blocks of stone, and have tiled roofs, they are thirty or forty feet in length, and some twenty feet in breadth. The gangway passes through the centre, and on each side are broad stone benches where people can sit, or recline at ease in the cool shade. Men are always to be found at these places, chatting, smoking, sleeping, or may be stitching; for the men do all the tailoring, even to sewing together lengths of cotton stuff, to make dresses for their wives; the women weave but do not use the needle. These covered resting-places may be considered as the centres of village politics, for every village is divided into different parties, each anxious to elect the Amine or chief, who has power to inflict fines up to a certain amount.

The word Jamâ, the Arabic for mosque, means simply the place of assembly. Friday is el Jemâa, the day of assembly, the Mohamedan Sunday. The Aïth Ménguellath market is called Souk-el Jemâa, Friday's market. The native name for Fort National is l'Arba, or the fourth day, a market being held there every Wednesday. Before French rule, the duty of the Amine in

times of peace was to maintain the tribal laws, in times of war he
commanded the fighting men, but only to carry out some plan
previously determined on by the Jemãa. When schemes of war
on an extensive scale had to be executed, the Amines of a tribe
chose a President, who commanded the united tribal force. Communal laws were collected into a complete code, called Kanoun ;
these varied in different tribes, but only on points of detail.   In
certain cases when these laws were unable to deal with new circumstances, the Jemãa was called together and a decree elaborated.
An account of the Kanoun is given by C. Devaux, also by le Baron
H. Aucapitaine (' Etude sur le passé et l'avenir des Kabyles ').
The latter says: ' The Kanouns, the repositories of the laws and
customs of the Kabyles, are interesting specimens of the political
constitution of the democratic Berbers. We have searched history in
vain for the origin of this democratic system, forming to-day the
base of Kabyle justice.'   Several writers have thought that the
word Kanoun is derived from the Greek word κανών, an opinion
justified, says Aucapitaine, by the name still given to codes in
vigour among the Greek Christians of Albania.   Among the
Miridites, justice is still administered after the ' Canounes Sech '
preserved by tradition.

The village chief is still chosen by the majority of votes of the
heads of families met together in council.   He is responsible to
the Kaïd, or President of the tribe, for the orderly conduct of the
village, and the President again is responsible to the Bureau Arabe
stationed at Fort National.   The administration of the country is
on the point of being changed from the military to civilians, a
vexed question about which I have nothing to say.   There is no

police of any sort among the tribes. On asking a native what
happens should a disturbance occur at night, or should a robbery
take place, he replied : ' All the men in the neighbourhood turn out
of their houses to assist in quieting matters and in securing the
suspected party; the following day there is a general talk and
investigation into the matter before the Amine.'

At the season when the figs are ripening, men keep watch in
their fields by night. Constructions of cane in the trees, looking
like huge nests, are to be seen, where men at that season pass the
night guarding the fruit.

In some parts of the country daring robbers, over whom the
Amine has no control, invade the plantations—Barbary apes, which
live among the high cliffs.

There are no shops in the villages. Were a man to open one,
I take it the Kabyles are too suspicious of being overcharged to
go in and buy. All the business of the country is done at the
markets, where there is a lively competition and everything is open
and discussable. Husbands, when at work, have the satisfaction
of knowing that their wives cannot squander their money in riotous
shopping ; at any rate, they like their system of doing things, and
mean to stick by it. Though the markets be distant, they like the
walk to them, the company, the talk by the way, the concourse of
many tribesmen, the news from distant quarters, the eager bargaining, the comparing of notes, the greetings of friends, the disputes
with enemies. Is it not all lively and amusing ? Above these
merits in my eyes, is it not extremely picturesque ?

From the open bit of ground between the villages of Ouarzin
and Taourirt the view of the Jurjura is magnificent. With the early

morning sun behind, the rocks throw great blue shadows, and are
superb in colour, their formation is limestone, moulded in the
grandest forms, the loftiest peak is 7,542 feet. The village of
Taourirt is a trifle above the level of Fort National. Owing to
the absence of glacial action, the general character and form of the
highest mountains recurs in a curious way throughout the country—
more or less obliterated, however, by the action of water. As some
peal of thunder may re-echo until the softened reverberations die
in silence, so do the forms of the lofty crags repeat, until with
elegant lingering curves they finally plant themselves with quiet
precision upon the dead level of the plain. On this open ground,
just mentioned, are four or five mills for crushing olives. These
are very simple in construction. A basin about twelve feet in diameter and three feet high is built of masonry, into this the olives
are poured. A heavy cross-beam supported at its extremities
by two others fixed vertically in the ground, passes over the
centre of the basin, and its object is to keep the grindstone in
its place, which is accomplished in the following manner. The
stone, in an upright position, works like a wheel round a pole
placed in the centre of the basin ; this pole revolves, turning in a
socket at its lower extremity, and in another above, attached to
the overhanging beam. To the centre of the grindstone a long
handle is fixed, men and women, pushing and pulling at this, run
round and round the basin, and making the stone roll in the
trough, which is lined with flat slabs ; it crushes the olives which
are placed in its way. It is about a foot in thickness, with the
edge slightly bevelled, to cause it to roll easily.

One of the mills had its stone dislodged and lying on its side.

This, of a reddish tinge tipped with bright light, looked like a mass of porphyry against the amethyst colour of the mountain shadows.

When olives are plentiful the gathering lasts for several months, beginning in October nor ending till February, and it is a charmingly picturesque sight. Men standing round a tree beat down the fruit with long wands, then they climb up to beat and shake the branches, till all the berries have fallen. ' As the shaking of an olive tree, two or three berries in the top of the uppermost bough, four or five in the outmost fruitful branches thereof,' is a Biblical simile for a small remnant. Upon a Greek vase in the British Museum, an olive tree is depicted being stripped of its fruit in the manner described.

Meanwhile the women are busy, working side by side, picking up the fallen fruit and putting it into baskets, which are emptied on to cloths spread on the ground. At close of day the heaped berries are poured into sacks, and carried up to the villages on mules.

The olive is the chief wealth of Kabylia; it grows in the greatest luxuriance. The lower slopes of the mountains are covered with it, and some miles distant from Borj Boghni, at the foot of the Jurjura, there is an especially grand old forest. The berries are left lying in a heap for some days, during which time they undergo a certain amount of fermentation. They are next poured into round shallow depressions in the ground, made in an exposed spot, sometimes they are placed on the roofs of the houses. Here the sun ripens and softens them to the uttermost, extracting by evaporation water contained in them,

and allowing the pulpy part to be easily disengaged from the
kernel. They now look all shiny with oil, are of the deepest
purple colour, and ready to be carried to the mill, where they are
crushed in the manner I have described :

> Then olives, ground in mills, their fatness boast.

The oil is extracted from the mass by pressure. A square
block of masonry about a yard in height, contains a stone basin at
the top of it, and a hole at the bottom of the basin allows the oil
running out to be collected. Flat bags of alfa grass, filled with
the crushed olives, are piled in the basin, a heavy flat piece of wood
placed on the top, and pressure is brought to bear, by means of a
wooden screw, which passes through a strong cross-beam, supported by two stout upright poles. The remains of the pressed
mass are carried to some stream, where holes about three feet deep
are arranged so that water from the stream can enter and afterwards be allowed to run off. When the holes are filled, the remains
of the olives are thrown in, the women tuck up their dresses
and jump in too, beating and knocking the mass about, and the
refuse dirty water is allowed to escape.

Soap is manufactured from the oily residue, by mixture with
wood ashes.

But to return from this digression. We went from Taourirt to
Tamjoot, about a mile distant and somewhat lower, on one of the
arms of the mountain. The rocky pathway passed through a
little open cemetery, where a beautiful group of cork and ash
formed a leafy bower above. In the background, the little
village appeared perched on a prominence, and the picture was

GATHERING OLIVES.

Like some fair olive, by my careful hand
He grew, he flourish'd, and adorn'd the land.
Pope's *Iliad*, Book xviii.

completed by the magnificent outline and precipices of the mountains.

We stood watching for some time groups of picturesque peasants issuing from the shade, and making their way to the market below; some, bearing goods done up in skins; some, earthenware pots netted together with twisted grass cords; others driving sheep and goats, asses and cattle. There is not much to be gained by entering the villages; they look best from the outside, and Tamjoot was not an exception to the rule. We halted at the Jamâ at the entrance, and a friendly Kabyle brought us clotted sour milk and figs, with which we refreshed ourselves. We returned by another path, overhung the greater part of the way with ash; the land was well cultivated with corn, and bore besides a profusion of fig-trees and evergreen oak. On arrival at the tent, we were glad to find that Dominique had not been inactive, and we did justice to his first 'déjeuner.'

Each mountain has its tribe—Qabíla is the Arabic word for tribe, Qabaïli, a tribesman—and the villages are all built on the crests. The reason for this is apparent from a mere glance at the country, the slopes are so extremely steep that there is no other place where they could easily be built, and the gorges are occupied only by the stony beds of torrents; the springs also are found generally not far from the summits. Such situations have the advantage of fine healthy air, free from fevers; and in unsettled times, before the French introduced regular government, they no doubt to a great extent afforded the inhabitants immunity from the attacks of their neighbours.

From all accounts, in the good old days, the tribes were constantly quarrelling, and thus found distraction from the monotony of a too uneventful existence.

The area of country enclosed between the sea and the Jurjura, is about 3,850 square miles. The number of armed men at the time of the conquest, has been estimated at 95,000. Reckoning a little less than three times as many women and children, gives a total of 350,000 souls, or the high rate of 90 per square mile.

No village shows any signs of fortifications, or preparations for defence. The deep gulf fixed between the mountains, practically keeps the different groups of villages far more separated from each other than if they were built on islands. Before the French occupation, the people used always to go about armed. C. Devaux, a captain of Zouaves, has thus described a fight in the old times ; it is full of picturesque suggestion :—

'In the case of a village not having a sufficient number of fighting men to hold the field, when about to be attacked by superior forces, the defenders hastened to arrange means of resistance. Trenches were dug and mounds raised, according to the position of the ground to be defended, the outlets of the streets were closed by walls of piled stones, and at the moment of attack, each man occupied the place assigned him.

'The women, young and old, joined in the fray ; in their gala dresses, bedecked with their jewellery, and holding each other's hands, they chanted a war-song, and from time to time raised thrilling cries to inflame the courage of the defenders. These songs, these war-cries of the women, heard in the midst of the fusillade, produce a most vivid effect. Having many times been called on to conduct Kabyle contingents at the defence of a village menaced by the enemy, I have felt, when I heard the exciting cries of the wives and mothers, how greatly they touch the fighting fibre of the combatants.

'Things are managed differently when the French attack ; then the women are sent into the mountains with the children and the flocks and herds ; for in case of the village being taken they would be made prisoners, whilst between Kabyles the women were always released, and in no instance was any insult offered them.'

I am afraid that when the French attacked, the women were not always so comfortably sent out of the way as this officer describes, and that they fared badly. One day an old soldier was abusing the Kabyle women to me. 'C'est incroyable,' said he, 'comment sont méchantes les femmes Kabyles.' I asked him to be kind enough to descend from generalities to particulars. He thereupon described an attack on a village, at which he had been present, when the women had assisted the men in the defence. He told me how, when the bullets were flying, he and a comrade had rushed at the doorway of one of the houses ; his friend, a few paces in advance, killed a Kabyle just as he was levelling his gun to fire ; but vengeance was instant, there was the flash of a pistol, his comrade fell dead ; rushing on, he made a plunge with his bayonet, and on withdrawing it, behold! he had run it through the body of the Kabyle's faithful wife. 'Vous voyez, monsieur,' he concluded, 'comment sont méchantes les femmes Kabyles.'

The extreme timidity of the women to this day, running away, as they often do, in the most idiotic manner on the first sight of a European, arises of course from their fears at the time of the war. It seems clear that in former times the fighting that occurred among the Kabyles was, as a rule, of a much milder nature than a war against an invader. They fought about points of honour, or personal dignity. When a tribe thought itself insulted by another and sought vengeance, it would send the young men to attack the flocks and herds, the animals taken in a *coup de main* were slaughtered and the meat distributed among the tribe.

From that moment they made ready for war. Skirmishing would begin; the marabouts, or priests, would then enter the field as conciliators, but as they knew from experience that by reasoning they would not succeed in extinguishing animosity, they tried to calm matters by making conditions, such as, that they should not fight at night, or that on such and such days fighting should be suspended. However, if one of the parties was greatly irritated by losses or insults, the voice of the marabouts was not listened to, and matters often became very serious; they would attack day or night at any hour, all communication was interrupted, they dug trenches, houses were burned, trees cut down, and, in short, they did all the harm they could. In the ordinary way the warriors of both sides betook themselves to the spot set apart by custom for finishing quarrels, and there fought in the manner of sharp-shooters. Each combatant sought to approach as near as possible, gliding from bush to bush; and when within easy range, his gun resting on the branch of a tree, or a stone, he would fire and then retire without troubling to see if he had hit.

When two Kabyles fight without weapons, they claw like wild cats, a disgusting way of fighting. Once during my stay in the tribe of the Zouardia, two men, close to where I was painting, began to fight about a boundary. A herdsman had driven his cows on to a pasture which he believed to be communal property; another man, meeting him, told him to walk off, because he himself only had a right over the land, having rented it of the commune. They forthwith began mauling and clawing at each other's faces; matters were becoming serious, and I had just sharpened my pencil to try and sketch them, when a third party at work near, separated them; they calmed down almost immediately, each rather pleased with himself at having shown that he was game to fight. On coming up to me, I tried to explain that in England men fought with the fist; thereupon they grinned good-naturedly. I have been shown an iron claw that is sometimes worn on the hand when fighting, a very nasty and dangerous weapon, answering to the American knuckleduster. The wagmuck, an iron claw fixed upon the hand, is an historical weapon of the Deccan. Sivajee, the founder of the Maharatta Empire, murdered Afzul Khan with it—an incident introduced by Colonel Meadows Taylor into his novel of Tara.

> So on the confines of adjoining grounds,
> Two stubborn swains, with blows, dispute their bounds;
> They tug, they sweat: but neither gain, nor yield
> One foot, one inch, of the contended field.

All the world has heard of the fighting qualities of the Kabyles under the name of Turcos. I have often talked with natives who took part in the Franco-German war, who have recounted to me their experiences of Sedan, their long journey into Germany, and how they nearly died of cold.

Though each mountain extends over a large area, the summit

is very limited; this is especially the case in the tribe of the Aïth Menguellath. In the afternoon we took a walk of exploration down the backbone of our mountain, we had gone but a few minutes, when we faced an eminence covered with clustered houses, and a short distance beyond was a second village-crowned knoll. A curious effect was caused by the shadows of trees cast in straight lines downwards upon the corn-covered slope, looking like reflections in a liquid sea of green, the extraordinary freshness of the colouring was heightened by the deep blue ranges beyond. Farther, we came upon an open space covered with tombs and evergreens.

At one end of this cemetery was a little white Kouba, or chapel, built over the tomb of a celebrated marabout, with coloured tiles round the doorway. It was shaded by a group of oaks, while on one side we caught a peep of the village set on the hill; one of these trees, which overhangs the path, has a quantity of little dirty bits of rag tied to the branches by women. It is not uncommon to come across some insignificant-looking bush covered with tatters; sometimes alongside is a niche made for a lamp, where simple offerings, such as a few handfuls of figs, are left. Certainly the bits of rag cannot be called offerings; they are left in recognition of the holy man buried there, equivalent to leaving a card in passing, an act at which no offence can possibly be taken, and which perchance may be regarded by the deceased as a pleasing attention. Hard by lives a marabout known to the people as Uncle Zaïd, an old man who looks after the chapel, and does a great deal of praying. We now found ourselves upon a grassy space, where shepherds pasturing their flocks were sitting under

MEETING.

The season now for calm, familiar talk,
Like youths and maidens in an evening walk.
                                 Pope's *Iliad*, Book xxii.

the shade of ilexes. Before us rose a steep ascent, crowded with a mass of lichened tombstones, of a beautiful warm grey ; and growing among them were ilexes, corks, and figs trained into leafy canopies above the graves, and pomegranates crimson with budding leaves. The hill was crowned by Thililit. Skirting the cemetery was a path among rocks, up and down which charming groups of women and girls, with pitchers on their heads, passed to and fro from the fountain ; unfortunately they were timid as deer, and on seeing us, fled in a scared way behind the shelter of trees, from which they peeped out spying, till we had passed. We walked through Thililit, and the path continued with equal interest beyond. Passing a little plateau, we arrived at the second village, that we had seen at a distance appearing above the first ; this was Aourir-Amer-ou-Zaïd. The ridge continued in a straight line half a mile further, and led to Iril Boghni, but we postponed a visit thither. We felt that another walk in this direction was imperative, if it were only for a chance of catching sight of a girl who was talking merrily with her neighbours at the door of her house in the village of Amer-ou-Zaïd. She certainly was the most beautiful girl we met in the country, rich-complexioned, dark-eyed, with handsome features, and a supple graceful figure. Alas ! we never saw her again. ‘O maiden with delicate features, thou resemblest Stamboul, for thou hast many admirers.’

CHAPTER II.

THE features of the landscape below Thililit combined so happily together from many points that, upon a second visit, we agreed this spot was as choice as the heart of painter could desire, and provided more subjects than we could grapple with.

On our walk, Uncle Zaïd, a benevolent, white-bearded gentleman, accosted us, and offered cakes. By and by, we met Père Voisin reading his breviary, who said there was much talk in the villages concerning us, and questionings as to what we had come for, why were we staring, why prying about the country in that way? Did not the pulling out of paper and pencils mean mischief? Were we not 'Géomètres' come to trace out new roads? and would they, the Kabyles, be forced to work on them? He told us he had reassured them, explaining that we were Englishmen, and had nothing to do with the Government.

Sunday, April 11, 1880.—It blew hard during the night, and there was a heavy fall of rain, it was cold too, so that the unprepared Dominique was half-frozen to death, and we, not having more clothes than were quite necessary for ourselves, were forced to borrow wraps from the Fathers. On waking, behold, we were in the clouds and drizzle, unable to see many yards, so we determined to mark Sunday in the time-honoured fashion, by lying late a-bed. It rained all day, and we left the tent, only to take a constitutional under umbrellas.

The evening was spent with the Fathers. Père Gerbouin lent us a pamphlet printed for private circulation, giving an interesting account of a French missionary expedition to the Equatorial Lakes. A Brother, whom I had known when staying, two years previously, in the tribe of the Zouardia, had taken part in this expedition, and they had just learned the news of his death, at which they much grieved ; nor was he the only victim, for several others had succumbed to privations and fevers. Père Gerbouin was very enthusiastic on the subject, and greatly wished to join a fresh expedition that is to start from Algiers for Lake Victoria. He would be the right man in the right place ; for besides his enthusiasm he is tough and strong. He thought it a disgrace, at a time when England and Protestants are making such exertions in this field of enterprise, that France and the Roman Catholic Church should lag behind. Evidently the cannibals will shortly be placed in the delicate position of having to choose between rival sects of the same religion.

The Père also told us of the privations they had to endure while their present school-house was being built; how winter had

E

overtaken them, and they had to live in huts in the snow. They
also recounted many odd stories about our neighbours, and of the
hard life led by the poor.

In Kabyle society, the social unit is the family. The posses-
sions of a family are held in common, and are administered by the
father; at his death, by the son deemed to be the most capable to
manage affairs. The gains of each member of the family are
joined in a common fund. The exclusion of women to inheritance
is the consequence of this organisation, for, if the daughters
inherited like their brothers, the division of goods would bring
about the dispersal of the family.

Polygamy is lawful, but unusual, for the Kabyles as a rule are too
poor to be able to afford more than one wife. The women all marry
as soon as they arrive at the age of puberty. There is no written
contract at marriage. A Taleb—that is to say, a man knowing
how to read—recites the first and fourth chapters of the Koran,
there is no other religious ceremony. Before parting with his
daughter, the father receives a certain sum, which varies according
to her age, beauty, and her qualifications for making a good house-
wife, and according to the means of her intended husband.
Sometimes part of the price is given in a provision of corn and
figs. The father gives his daughter as a marriage portion a girdle
and jewellery ; these become her personal property, which no man
can take from her. If the father has received the price of his
daughter, and she should happen to die before the consummation of
marriage, he retains the money. If the husband die, leaving
his widow childless, she returns to her father, who marries her
again as he pleases. If she have children, her father cannot

give her in marriage without her consent; and if she pay him an
equivalent to what he would expect to receive from a man desiring
marriage with her, she becomes free from all paternal restraint.
This money is kept in trust for her children. If she marry, her
husband, who has had nothing to pay, engages to take care of the
children, who remain in the house with their mother. If a woman
refuse to live with her husband, she returns to the paternal roof,
when she becomes known as a 'rebel.' The husband still has
rights, and can forbid her marrying anyone else; he may allow
her to do so, provided the father consent, in which case the latter
receives the supplementary sum to be paid. A widow can only
re-marry after mourning four months and ten days; a divorced
woman must wait three months. A man having repudiated his
wife cannot take her back without paying again, and having the
marriage ceremony re-performed. In case of separation, the
children are brought up by the father.

Conjugal infidelity has to be avenged with blood. In the Beni
Ienni I heard of several cases of savage murder from this cause.

Two brothers, one of twenty, the other fifteen, having constantly been about the tent since our arrival, we engaged the
younger, who was very anxious to make himself useful, and knew
a few words of French, to do little commissions. Kabyle verbs
have an habitual form. As the elder was an adept in putting into
practice the verb to 'loaf,' we nicknamed him the habitual loafer.
We now learned with astonishment that the habitual loafer had
just taken to himself a second wife. Having no ready money, in
order to obtain one, he had offered the parents of the girl to whose
hand he aspired, a patch of land in pledge, until he should be able

to pay off the debt. After two months of troubled married life
he sent the girl back to her parents, I know not upon what plea.
These naturally claimed the field, but the youth's mother (his
father was dead) brought proof that the land had been given to
her. The returned girl got no recompense, though free to marry
again. The late husband began making fresh advances to another
girl. Number two took better precautions ; moreover, the habitual-
loafer promised to earn a certain sum of ready money before
marriage, and he started to seek his fortune in Algiers. After
a three months' absence, he turned up with thirty sous in his
pocket ; the young lady however was not *difficile*, and with an
eye perhaps on the land—it could not have been on her lover—
accepted him in spite of his meagre success.

Some of the well-to-do natives engage private instructors to
teach their sons Arabic and the Koran, but this is rare ; such a
teacher is living in the village of Thililit, where he conducts a
school. Reclining under the shade of the ilexes, we heard the
voices of the children chanting the Koran, a native by our side,
perceiving how our attention was occupied, pointing in that direction, said, ' Kief kief Afrouken ' (just like the birds). When
Kabyle is written, the Arabic characters are adopted. Among
the Touaregs, a Berber people more to the south, an indigenous
alphabet is in use. General Hanoteau translates some sentences
thus written, which were inscribed by a woman on the shield
of a Touareg chief. The writing is from right to left, and de-
cipherment is complicated by the omission of vowels, and of
divisions between words. Poor vowels, they often fare badly.
Even in ordinary Arabic writing they are much snubbed, treated

as superfluous luxuries, and hustled out of the way by self-
sufficient consonants, and never meet with the frank recognition due to their merit.   In the Koran they certainly fare
better, everything is as perfect as possible, and all vowels are
introduced, but even then they are poor little things above and
below the line, attendant upon a sturdy row of consonants.   In
the cellars of the British Museum are a few ancient Lybian
inscriptions.   There is one bilingual stone, Phœnician and Berber.
This ancient Berber writing is almost identical with that still in
use among the Touaregs.

Monday, April 12, 1880.—Another wet morning and dense
mist.   I occupied myself with studying Kabyle.   Before leaving
Algiers, M. Stora, a Jew, ' interprète à la cour d'assise,' gave me a
few lessons, the only man of education I could hear of, who had
knowledge of the language.   I paid him about a dozen short visits,
when he kindly gave me all the assistance he could.   I also carried
with me a Kabyle grammar, written some years ago by General
M. Hanoteau, and a French and Kabyle dictionary, compiled by
the Jesuits, which proved most useful.

The ignorance of the French concerning the language is remarkable, considering the large Berber population they have to
govern.   I believe there are some half-dozen Europeans at Fort
National with some smattering, but the only Europeans who
thoroughly understand it are the Fathers.

The colonists, forced into contact with the natives, get into the
habit of speaking a debased pidgin language, a mixture of bad
Arabic, French, and Spanish, but sometimes they do not even
attain this.   For instance, Mme. Pierre at Fort National has

kept an hotel there for twenty-five years, and has dealings with
the natives at all hours; she does not know a single word of
Kabyle, nor can she put together a single sentence in Arabic.
When 'colons' cannot make the natives understand, the 'cochons
d'indigènes' are in fault for not learning French. Our man
Dominique was a spirit of this nature; he had roughed it for
years amongst an Arab population in the province of Oran; to
the best of my belief, his stock of Arabic consists in the magic
words 'Goul' and 'Jib hadda,' by which he means to express
'take' and 'bring that.' On arrival among the mountains, he
remarked, 'Ici on parle arabe avec un dialecte très différent de celui
d'Alger.' I doubt whether, on leaving the country, he was aware
that they spoke a language altogether distinct from Arabic. As an
instance of his incapacity for picking it up: he took in fresh milk
for our breakfast daily during two months and a half; the last morning he was with me, after removing to another tribe, when in bed,
I was amused to overhear him vainly striving to express his desire
for milk, but unable to make the puzzled native understand.

The weather gradually cleared; we sallied out in good spirits,
and planted our easels at the foot of the cemetery of Thililit. We
were quickly surrounded by a little crowd, who sat down to watch
our proceedings, and remained the whole afternoon chatting good-
humouredly. Having discovered their mistake in believing us to
be agents of Government come to trouble them in some way, they
now seemed to be very pleased, and kept repeating 'Inglese
buono,' 'Français,' then they shook their heads, and spoke
earnestly. We in our turn took to shaking our heads, and the
Kabyles seemed disappointed that we could not understand them.

In civilised countries, if curiosity should bring a spectator to a painter's side, he would probably say to himself after a while, 'Now I must not waste time, I must be off and do something.' In the more easy-going south, a Kabyle so placed would more probably say to himself, 'Ah! here's an opportunity for a new occupation, to watch this man.'

Tuesday, April 13, 1880.—It blew mightily during the night, the wind roaring in the gulf beneath, and rushing over the crest on which our tent was pitched, canvas shook and pole trembled; and the possibility of tent-pegs being drawn, or cords snapping, caused us unpleasant reflections. On waking in the morning, we found a group of Kabyles waiting outside. They brought four handsome women's garments, and bargaining began, which ended in our buying these dresses cheaply, considering the labour bestowed upon them. 'It is naught, it is naught, saith the buyer; but when he is gone his way, then he boasteth.'

Besides satisfaction in possessing these cloths as costumes, we found them serviceable as warm coverlets, and were able to return the wraps we had borrowed; of this we were glad, thinking that the Fathers had none too many for themselves.

The Amine or village chief of Taourirt, next made his appearance with some friends to offer hospitality, saying that, if agreeable, he would send us a kouskous that evening. We thanked him, and said we should be very pleased; he had hardly departed when the Amine of Ouarzin, approaching, offered us the hospitality of his village, another kouskous for mid-day. We got one of the schoolboys to explain, if it were agreeable to him, we should like it deferred, thinking it impossible to eat two mountains of

kouskous. The Ouarzinites were not going to be cut out in that
fashion, so we had to accept; before mid-day the dishes appeared.
The company consisted of the Amine and some of the village
counsellors, and three marabouts; there was a large bowl containing the kouskous well piled up, a boiled fowl, with a jug of
sauce, another full of sour milk, a dish of boiled eggs, delicious
honey, and dried figs. Kouskous is wheat ground roughly;
two women grind it, sitting on the ground facing each other.
The appropriateness of the Biblical saying is then apparent ('two
women shall be grinding at the mill, the one shall be taken and the
other left'). Water-mills are also constructed on some of the
streams. The flour is slightly moistened, passed through a sieve,
and rolled out with the hand till it takes the form of little balls
about the size of fine shot; this is boiled, moistened with gravy,
and seasoned with pepper. Like macaroni, it is a wholesome
satisfying dish. Placed in the midst of the company, each guest
is served with a round wooden spoon, with which he attacks the
heap, gravy is constantly poured on; in eating the chicken, he
has to make use of his fingers.

The Pères joined in the meal; with their help we were able to
follow the conversation. A discussion arose between the two
principal marabouts, as to whether photography and the painting
of portraits is 'hareem,' 'a thing prohibited;' the elder, the more
liberal-minded, contended that there was no harm in the matter,
the other declared that there was; the elder, being a Hadj, was
voted to have most authority. The third marabout, a man with
light-coloured hair and dull expression, had nothing to say. I
think kouskous must have got into his head. One of the Amine's

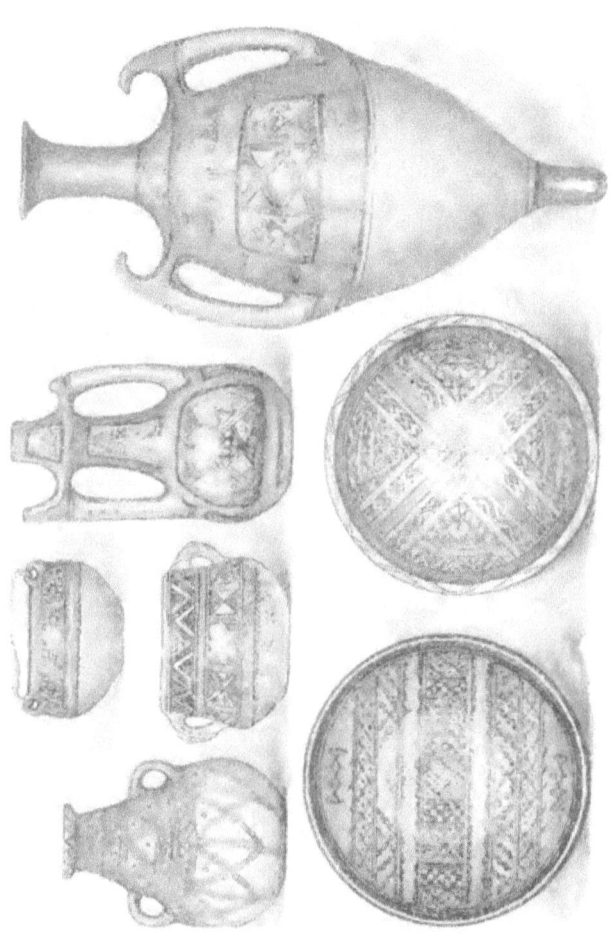

friends started the opinion that if a man possessed the portrait of another he also possessed a power to work him mischief ; though he could not say he believed it himself, others did ; might there not be some truth at the bottom of the notion ? Was it proved certainly false that if one man bearing malice were to bury another's portrait, the original of the likeness would sicken and die ? This belief was much ridiculed, though they had all heard it before. We expressed regret at not having our cartes-de-visite to offer, that he might plant them in his garden.

When we had finished, the dishes were handed to Dominique, who served himself, while muttering his disgust at native cookery. The rest then made a circle, and the remaining provisions were quickly disposed of.

After the feast, we took a walk to Iril Boghni, the last village on the backbone of the mountain. On the way we had to pass the house where lived the beautiful girl ; we hoped to catch sight of her, but the door was shut, and she would not come out. A Kabyle was sitting at the corner carving wooden spoons with an adze ; we took the greatest interest in his occupation, and stood a long time watching ; it was no good, the rude envious door was determined not to change the direction of its face, and hid the beauty from us. On our way back I made a great effort to converse in Kabyle with a man who addressed us. He seemed amused—I dare say with good reason—but politely invited us to step into his house. I thought he was making straight for the home of the beautiful girl—how attentive of him!—no, unluckily it was the next house that he entered.

We sat down at the entrance of a dark smoky room. He

spoke to a woman, who rose from her seat behind a loom ; she went
out and brought in milk and figs ; resuming her work, the busy
fingers were alone distinct, the threads of the loom forming a thin
veil before her figure.   This humble-minded artist was weaving a
dress with elaborate patterns ; yet she had no design before her
to help, and moreover had to manufacture her own machine and
arrange the threads.   I was astonished at the simplicity of the
loom ; the warp was fixed in an upright frame made out of
canes ; she used no shuttle, but passed the woof from side to side
with her fingers, and jammed it home tight with a metal hand-
comb, a most laborious method of weaving.   But because the
mechanical means were rude, let not the reader imagine that the
work was so, for exactly the reverse is the truth.   She brought an
old dress made some years before, much used, but most beautiful
in workmanship, design, and colour—indeed, as a piece of colour it
excelled all other woven cloths that we saw in that part of the
country.   I made her understand that I had bought some dresses,
and that I should like to possess that one, but she seemed loath to
part with it.   'Give her of the fruit of her hands, and let her own
works praise her in the gates.'   'She is not afraid of the snow for
her household, for all her household are clothed with double garments.'   She was past middle age, and strength and sight
seemed to be failing ; she had lost the sight of one eye, sitting ever
working in that smoky atmosphere.   A young and comely woman,
probably her daughter, tended a sleeping babe, gently swinging its
cradle slung from a beam in the roof.

> So from her babe, when slumber seals his eye,
> The watchful mother wafts th' envenom'd fly.

As I watched the figure of the weaver, distinct or half lost according as it approached or receded from the web before it, while the busy fingers peeped out now here, now there, moving ceaselessly, I was reminded of the description of the handmaids in the Palace of Alcinous :

> Some ply the loom ; their busy fingers move
> Like poplar leaves when Zephyr fans the grove.

I could not help contrasting her with those ladies at home who take part in the movement for Art needlework. I also unsuccessfully attempted to learn the nature of the dyes employed, and was shown some mysterious gummy substances. I could not understand a word of what the good woman said, but am under the impression that she must have been explaining that they were ' Art colours.'

Let it be here remarked, that the women's dresses are not dresses at all in the sense of being garments made up, or cut out ; they are simply pieces of drapery disposed about the body, fastened beneath the shoulders with brooches, and confined at the waist with a girdle ; but for the girdle and the overlapping of the edges of the cloth, the wearer's person would be disclosed on one side. The width of the loom is the same as the measure from the chin to the ground. This given, weaving is continued until the cloth is completed ; the length usually being twice the width ; but sometimes they are made twice as long, giving a double thickness when worn. Shorter pieces are also woven, an extra protection for the back ; these are fastened to the shoulder-pins, and confined by the girdle, but show the underdress about the bosom, and for a few inches above the ankles. When the wearer sits down, this extra piece is seen enveloping the thighs and knees, while the underdress droops through below, in the way so often represented in Greek statues and bas-reliefs. Formerly I used to regard this arrangement as simply an agreeable artistic device, for allowing the folds of the outer garment to contrast with those below; it was not until I visited Kabylia, that I perceived that its true *raison d'être* was protection for the back. Before returning, we went to watch the women draw water at the fountain. There were groups of fine women showing well-rounded arms and necks, as they walked in a stately way with Greek-looking vases on their heads.

> The liquid crystal fills their polish'd urns ;
> Each nymph exulting to the town returns.

Many of these handsome girls could not, I think, be distinguished from Italians, if transported to San Germano or Atina, and dressed like Italian peasants ; but the majority are of course not handsome, and there is a type of countenance which is peculiar, as though there might be some admixture of Tartar blood—broad faces with marked cheek-bones, and thickish lips. Their hair is always of a raven black; I imagine they sometimes add that which they think nature lacks, because the men are not all dark-haired. The colour that warms the cheeks of these brunette beauties is also sometimes due to feminine art.

The men have good-shaped heads and marked features ; before middle age they are strongly bronzed, furrowed, and rugged ; most wear black moustachios and beards ; now and then one will be found with hair as red as any Scotchman's. There is undoubtedly more variety than amongst the Arabs. The Arab has a high prominent nose, with a droop in the line of the nostril, like Dante's nose; full projecting lips and invariable black hair. The Kabyle is wanting in all this; he is lower of stature, but has more expression of countenance. Unfortunately, the children have not the delicate beauty comparable to what one sees in an Arab town like Tlemcen.

At evening came our second kouskous from hospitable Taourirt. When all was finished, we handed round cups of tea—a beverage the Kabyles were not acquainted with, and appreciated; at dusk they took their departure.

The wind during the afternoon had dropped, but the atmosphere was ominously murky and sultry, the mountains barely visible, patches of snow on their summits just showing above their shadowy bodies. When the Kabyles left, the wind was rapidly rising, while a black dangerous-looking cloud stretched itself from one horizon to the other, the sky on either side remaining clear.

Wednesday, April 14, 1880.—What a night this was a prelude to! Soon the wind, straight from the tops of the Jurjura, came rushing and raging over the abyss below, and shook our tent, as if it were a leaf on the point of parting from its bough. About midnight there was a lull; we hoped that the worst was past. No; we had as yet been treated only to the overture; the winds, which seemed to have been collecting and gathering evil strength in the valleys, suddenly rushed onwards again like wild beasts determined to destroy us, roaring as they swept in fury through the trees. I never heard such a storm, and we were sorely afraid that no tent could stand it for long; sleep was out of the question, we sat up all night ready against any emergency, for we

dreaded a catastrophe every moment. The central support was
made of iron tubing, with a cap at the top; this latter was carried
away early in the evening—a mishap that let in the wind between
the canvas and the lining; some of the attachments gave way,
and the lining flapped in an ungovernable manner. When it
became light enough to examine, we found most of the wooden
pegs pulled out of the ground, and the ropes fastened to grave-
stones broken; six long irons only, driven in up to their heads,
remained firm and had saved us.   Thankful we were that the tent
was standing; it had stuck on bravely to the mountain, like a
limpet to a rock, when the rising waves rush over it.   It was a
sirocco not to be forgotten.   'As whirlwinds in the south pass
through, so it cometh from the desert, from a terrible land.'
Later in the day, the wind somewhat abated in its fury, but we
remained in the tent, glad to take some repose.

In the afternoon we searched for a fresh camping-ground, as it
was impossible to remain in safety where we were; this was not
easy to find, uncultivated land being restricted, and not sufficiently
level.   We concluded that there was only one practicable spot, the
corner of a fallow field, thoroughly protected from the sirocco by
the hill; the next thing was to get permission to camp there.

Père Voisin good-naturedly helped us.   The owner of the field
was absent, but the Amine of Ouarzin gave leave, saying no one
would disturb us.   This settled, we lost no time; a party of
Kabyles came down to lend help; half-an-hour later all our effects
were transported on their backs to the spot, and as night fell, the
tent was well pitched in its new position, and the fire lit to prepare
our evening meal.   On turning into bed, we congratulated our-

selves, for we heard the tempest, howling and raging with renewed fury, above; but before reaching us its strength was broken and lost in the surrounding trees, and the tent remained in peace and quiet.

Thursday, April 15, 1880.—Several paths converged at the point where we now found ourselves, the most frequented being a steep lane leading to the fountain. It was shaded by trees whose branches interlaced elegantly with pretty peeps on to the distance; from the entrance to our tent we looked straight down this lane, towards the spring about two hundred yards off. The word 'spring' would suggest to most people simply water bubbling up and running off in a diminutive stream; a better word to use in this instance is 'fountain,' the French 'fontaine,' which has a different meaning to 'spring,' 'source'—inasmuch as it implies a basin, artificial or natural, combined with a natural welling-up of water. Unfortunately, the word 'fountain' is applied also to contrivances by which water is made to spout, the French 'jet d'eau.' The Kabyle fountain in question is a natural spring rising in the centre of a basin inclosed in a rude architectural structure, having a double arched entrance and gabled roof. The water is thus protected from dirt, dust, and the heat of the sun. By the side where the women fill their pots is a second structure, much dilapidated, reserved for the watering of beasts. The overflow is conducted into a basin where the women wash clothes, and then runs gurgling down the mountain-side. In an embowered nook, where there are neat terraced beds of vegetables, little gutters are arranged, so that at the end of the day the overflow can be conducted there; when the bed nearest the fountain has been saturated, the water is blocked off from the first trench with a spadeful of earth, runs on to refresh the next, and so on till all the garden has drunk its fill ; when the rivulet, having done its work, regains its liberty.

> So when a peasant to his garden brings
> Soft rills of water from the bubbling springs,
> And calls the floods from high to bless his bowers,
> And feed with pregnant streams the plants and flowers ;
> Soon as he clears whate'er their passage stay'd,
> And marks the future current with his spade,
> Swift o'er the rolling pebbles, down the hills,
> Louder and louder purl the falling rills.

I had not to wander far to find a subject for painting, and lost no time in getting to work in the lane. A bewildering number of interesting groups kept passing ; women and girls bearing pitchers, classical-looking herdsmen, driving sheep and goats, little kids, calves, and heifers ; and husbandmen would go by with mules and donkeys, on their way to till the land, or to hew and collect firewood.

Soon the path was blocked with people declaring that I was in everybody's way, and that I could not remain there painting ; for the women said (so I gathered from a man who spoke a few words of French) that they were afraid to pass, being especially alarmed at my umbrella. This was too ridiculous ; though the umbrella was certainly large, I considered it too useful to be put on one side, or indeed to be treated slightingly.

One morning, when passing through the market-place in Algiers, I had noticed a man selling jewellery under an enormous umbrella ; it struck me that such a one would suit me exactly for painting. Admiring its noble proportions, I went up and

spoke to the owner, who obligingly left his stall in charge of a
friend, and introduced me to the maker. I forthwith ordered
another. It was made to take to pieces—each rib about four
feet long, and practically, it was more serviceable than a small tent.
It had a big iron spike, which could be rammed into the ground
almost anywhere ; it could besides be steadied with guys ; it was
large enough to shade me and my work, and it had a cover impervious to light ; moreover, I could unloop the cover from the
ends of the rods, and roll it up, so that without difficulty I could
let in light in whatever direction I pleased. I was determined
not to desert such an umbrella for all the women of Kabylia, so
I let the men talk and gesticulate, and went on painting as if I
heard them not.

When Muirhead returned, I beat an orderly retreat, to
'déjeuner.' He too had had his trials, being quite baffled by the
strong wind, which swept over the crest where Uncle Zaïd's
kouba stands.

When painting under my umbrella, I found the cattle of
Kabylia even more timid than the fair sex. The cows are
small but nimble, the unusual appearance of a European is sufficient to scare them, and the umbrella added was altogether too
much for their nerves ; they would canter off gaily, to the conster-
nation of the herdsmen, shortly reappearing in order to eye me
warily. I stood as close as possible against the bank, keeping quiet,
when suddenly there was a rush, and the cows scampered by
in wild alarm at the frightful object. Instead of scowling and
muttering curses, as I expected and considered my due, the cow-
herd always stopped and greeted me in friendly fashion, sometimes

pressing upon me a handful of figs, as though I had done him a
favour.   Perhaps he thought that friendly demeanour made amends
for the ridiculous behaviour of his animals.   At first I regretted
causing all this trouble, and tried to express myself to that effect ;
after a time, discovering that they did not consider me to be a
more obnoxious animal than the gadflies, which abound, I continued to paint with equanimity, glad to be looked upon as a
natural evil.

After 'déjeuner,' two Fathers and a number of Kabyles paid us
a visit.   There were complaints of our tent being pitched close
to the road where the women were obliged to pass ; and words
began to flow apace.

The Amine of Ouarzin (or the Ogre) having given us permission to camp there, the Ogres had nothing to say, but the people
of the larger village of Taourirt en Taïdith (the Mount of the
Dog) doggedly objected.   They offered even to level a piece of
ground, and transport our tent and luggage free of expense, if we
would only move from the road.   Through the good words and
banter of the Fathers, 'the Dogs' at last left off barking, smiles
took the place of frowns, ruffled feelings were composed, and a
compromise effected.   We remained on the conditions that we
would leave the lane free between the hours of ten and four; and
that we would send a native lad to the fountain in place of
Dominique, who was to go no more at all, either to draw water or
wash clothes, except at a little-used spring pointed out ; to our dis-
may, a mere duckweed-covered puddle.   So the storm was lulled.

Friday, April 16, 1880.—I awoke, hearing the lively chatter of
women.   What a chirping there was !   They spoke in a very high

pitch of voice, and the language, as pronounced by them, sounded very different to that of the men. I peeped as discreetly as I could out of the tent, and behold! the lane was thronged; there were scores of them going to and fro, each with a pitcher on her head.

Alas! for the weather. The sirocco had been succeeded by a cold wind from the north, and the air was full of fog, it rained all day, and resembled more the climate of the Highlands of Scotland than what we anticipated the climate of North Africa would be.

We occupied ourselves with letter writing, reading, and trying to learn Kabyle, making persistent and comical attempts at conversation with natives who came to visit us; they were most inquisitive, but well-mannered, and anxious to talk. School hours over, the lads came to see us, pleased to air their stock of French, and equally eager to teach us words in Kabyle; this was just what we wanted, and we were soon excellent friends.

Saturday, April 17, 1880.—To-day proved more spring-like. I remained unmolested in the lane, whilst Muirhead went off to the Kouba. Uncle Zaïd always behaved to Muirhead as an uncle should, presenting him every day with clotted milk, hard-boiled eggs, cakes and figs; he always refused payment, shook his head, smiled blandly, pointed upwards with his forefinger, turned up his eyes, and ejaculated 'Errebbi, Errebbi!' (God, God!) to indicate that he acted thus merely to please the Almighty; let us hope that he behaves as well to all poor folk who cross his picturesque hill. We retaliated by giving dinner to his son and grandson, who came once or twice to the tent; but the little chapel received no

donation from us.   We continued our painting also at Thililit, and
Thililit vied with Ouarzin and Taourirt in hospitality to the
stranger.   The Amine, a fine-looking man, with an agreeable
countenance, offered us a kouskous.   We feared it would be
hopelessly cold before arriving at the tent ; but it was so well
wrapped up, that after a mile long journey it remained hot.   To-
day the Kaïd, or President of the Aïth Ménguellath, came over
from Fort National on business.   He called during our absence,
and left a message with Dominique, that if the natives annoyed
us, we were to complain to him.   After this, we went where we
would without interference.

SOWING.

And naked sow the land,
For lazy winter numbs the lab'ring hand.
DRYDEN's *Virgil*, Georgic 1.

CHAPTER III.

Sunday, April 18, to Thursday, April 22, 1880.

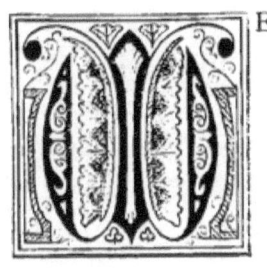E commenced fresh studies in a rocky ravine beneath Thililit, where trees nodded over the steep path. These sketches were never finished to our satisfaction, we were harassed by the sun, and continual calls to make way for brushwood-bearing peasants, timid cows, sheep, goats and kids. Much as I delight in goats and kids, they are truly provoking when they roll down stones upon one's picture, or skip into the palette.

Provisions are cheap, twelve fresh eggs for nine sous, for two sous more dried figs than can be piled in the hands. Every morning a lad brought us a freshly-baked wheaten loaf, unleavened, in the form of a round flat cake; we found this sweet and good, and ate it with honey. The more general bread of the people is made of barley-flour, but the sweet acorn of the ilex is also much used, and the natives think this as good as barley-flour, and pay as much for it. The poor are often reduced to a dinner of herbs; everyday we saw women washing salads; one in particular we noticed, that looked like celery, but which really was the midrib of the leaf of a thistle.

One morning a sportsman brought in a fat young boar that he had shot in the valley beneath, we gave him ten francs for it, an extravagant price, we learned afterwards. We presented the Fathers with half the meat, and there remained as much as we could dispose of. Dominique cooked well for us, but the contempt he entertained for all things native was sometimes annoying; he professed himself unable to swallow Kabyle bread, he said it made him ill; we always therefore supplied him with French bread, from Fort National, though we never ate it ourselves.

He is a fair specimen of a colonist, and abuses the natives in unmeasured terms. How would the *colons* get on without *les cochons d'indigènes?* The former exist by first getting the Government to give them a ' concession' of cultivated land belonging to the ' indigène,' and then employing the ex-proprietor to work for them. The most flattering expression I ever heard a Frenchman use towards the Kabyles was, ' une race capable d'être assimilée.' He doubtless thought this praise in the highest degree; but the remark was not altogether free from French conceit, nor true, except in the sense that a good beefsteak is assimilated when swallowed by a man of large appetite and strong digestion.

Muirhead had been expecting for some days, a visit from his friend W. B. R——, who had been spending the winter in Algiers, and from H. M——, on a holiday trip from Gibraltar. On April 22, the two appeared, having come from the Fort to reconnoitre before bringing their tent. They decided to pitch alongside of us, and shortly started on their way back.

Friday, April 23, 1880.—We went to the market Souk-el-Jemāa, the largest in the country, being held in the very heart of Kabylia, at a point central for populous tribes ; from one spot, thirty villages can be counted on the adjacent hills. It was an interesting walk, and there was again cause for wonder to find gradients so steep carefully cultivated. The Kabyles

> Let no spot of idle earth be found,
> But cultivate the genius of the ground.

The ash, plentiful about the summit, is prized by the people, not for the beauty of the trees, nor for the grateful shade they cast over the paths, but because their leaves afford forage during summer heats, when all herbage is parched. The boughs are lopped to cause a number of small branches to shoot out, and thus increase the quantity of leaves.

The fig plantations yield a most important harvest, dried figs being one of the staple foods of the country. The trees were in their most charming state, the beautiful mystery of silver-tangled stems not obscured, but enhanced by the golden sprinkling of opening leaves.

> In spring, when first the crow
> Imprinting, with light step, the sands below,
> So many thinly scatter'd leaves are seen
> To clothe the fig-tree's top with tender green.

The first-formed fruit drops off when half grown, to make place for that which is to arrive at maturity. When at Fort National last winter, I noticed dried figs hanging by threads from the branches, I was informed these were wild ones, and that minute insects escape, aiding the fructification of the plants from which they are suspended ; the Kabyles count thirty-two varieties of this tree. Ilexes too were in full flower, with green bronze-coloured tassels hanging in profusion. Not very dissimilar in appearance were the cork trees, sober but refined in colour, combining a certain quaintness with elegance of form. Vines everywhere twined in great serpentine lines amongst the foliage. Lastly, on the lower slopes were fine groves of olive ; a tree which grows with a vigour unmatched in Italy.

We scrambled down steep paths, and found ourselves at the foot of the mountain ; halting on a grassy slope, we heard the rush of a torrent in its stony bed, mixed with the hum of voices of many people, and looking over the edge of the slope, saw the market just beneath. There, Kabyles were closely packed, like a swarm of bees, and hundreds of white burnouses jostled among the olives. Rows of rustic bowers were used as shops. In the centre was a fountain for men, while the stream served for watering the animals ; on its banks flocks and herds were collected, and many animals had already been slaughtered for the day's consumption. In the market all the commodities that Kabyles have need of were for sale. Here were great piles of bowls and other utensils in wood ; there all sorts of earthenware vessels ; in other quarters, burnouses and articles of clothing, oil, figs, grain, skins, tobacco leaves, and many other things. At every step there were varying pictures ; but the heat was great, and in spite of the interest of the scene, we were soon glad to repose in the shade apart from the throng, where we lunched, and I spent the rest of the day painting and taking photographs. Besides supplying ourselves with meat and necessaries, I bought a woman's dress of singular design, splashed in a curious way with patches of red ; I also got pieces of cowhide, which were made up next day into sandals, which are called ercassen. The women usually do not attend the markets ; a few however can sometimes be seen in a knot by themselves with pottery for sale.

As we returned the Jurjura were almost obscured in mist, a sure sign of approaching sirocco ; the paths were crowded with peasants on their way home, in good humour, well satisfied with their day's bargaining.

Kabyle paths are abrupt and rugged in the extreme ; now running up over masses of rock, a very knife-edge of the mountain ; now in steps passing between deep banks overgrown with ferns and flowers ; one moment darkened by overhanging trees, an instant after they open upon a grand panorama, to twist again suddenly into some romantic bower. As we approached our tent at dusk, there by the side of it, was a second one, an army bell-tent, our friends having arrived during our absence.

Saturday, April 24 to *Tuesday, May* 4, 1880.—These were the days that they remained with us, most unfortunate as regards the weather, for we were often enveloped in dense cloud, and could see nothing.

> Swift gliding mists the dusky hills invade,
> To thieves more grateful than the midnight shade ;
> While scarce the swains their feeding flocks survey,
> Lost and confus'd amidst the thicken'd day.

So steamy was the air, that we hardly once saw the summits of the higher mountains. A furious sirocco was succeeded by a short ominous stillness, then a storm from the north enveloped us anew in cloud, and opened the flood-gates of heaven to an accompaniment of thunder and lightning; then a lull, to be followed by another storm and mist and drizzle, till everything was saturated. During these doubtful lulls, with breaks in the clouds as if it meant better things, we rambled, for the sake of exercise, and to see what we could of the country.

> When th' embattled clouds, in dark array,
> Along the skies their gloomy lines display,
> When now the North his boisterous rage has spent,
> And peaceful sleeps the liquid element,
> The low-hung vapours, motionless and still,
> Rest on the summits of the shaded hill
> Till the mass scatters as the winds arise,
> Dispers'd and broken, through the rufiled skies.

More thunder-storms, more hopeful breaks, when, towards evening, the sun would sink in golden glory beneath a troubled sea of purple mountains, and tinge the phalanxed clouds with gorgeous colours.

> So when thick clouds enwrap the mountain's head,
> O'er heaven's expanse like one black ceiling spread;
> Sudden the Thunderer, with a flashing ray,
> Bursts through the darkness, and lets down the day.
> The hills shine out, the rocks in prospect rise,
> And streams, and vales, and forests strike the eyes;
> The smiling scene wide opens to the sight,
> And all th' immeasur'd ether flames with light.

Thus would the declining sun shed rich gleams over wet grass and dripping foliage. Near the tents, in a secluded corner, an ilex on a knoll bent over an elegant ash, and a vine lovingly entwined among their branches, spangled with its leaves the ilex's sombre mass as with gems of translucent green. Hard by, a warning to the fated trees, a huge vine ungratefully strangled with its coils the aged ash which had for so many years supported it.

During these days the Kabyles came in numbers to the tents, bringing dresses and jewellery for sale; there was lively bargaining, and we made many purchases.

Before the French came, there were no cotton dresses: these have now become common, but the native woollen cloth is still usually worn.

The men's dress consists of a woollen tunic, confined at the waist with a belt, and a burnous; on the head is a close-fitting skull-cap, much like those worn by monks; added to this, in the summer time, is a plaited grass hat, very high in the crown, and with a huge brim, which falls into picturesque lines when the hat is old and battered; sandals complete the costume, though men often go barefoot as well as bare-headed. They crop the hair short, for Kabyles are not so careful about shaving as the Arabs.

The burnous is a white woollen cloak with a hood; it is closely woven, is durable, and impervious to heat and cold; an admirable piece of dress, designed with thorough good sense, and suited perfectly to the habits and requirements of the people. Its make is shown in the diagram, which supposes the cloak doubled and laid out flat on the ground. It then forms a quarter of a circle, of which the radius is the length from the neck to the ankle of the wearer, *a b.* The width of an ample hood is added along one side, and the hood itself forms a square in addition. The three strongly marked lines, A, B, C, show where it is closed. At A, the cloth is doubled, at ʙ and c it is sewn together. From this it will be understood that it is a garment woven all in one piece; no stuff has to be cut off, and thus no labour is wasted in its manufacture.

The tunic or shirt, if doubled and laid out in the same way, forms simply an oblong figure, with holes for the head and arms, and open below.

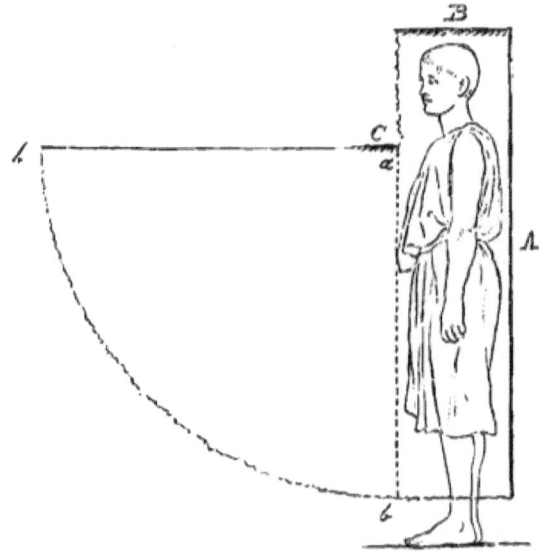

The burnous is worn in a multitude of ways. One of the ends hanging down in front is thrown across the breast and over the shoulder; or both sides are shortened, by being thrown up on the shoulders; or the cloak, suspended from one shoulder, is passed round the back, across the breast, and tucked under the armpit. Sometimes the hood muffles the head, sometimes it is thrown back, or the seam beneath the chin is put back to the nape of the neck,

while one elbow rests in the hood, which then plays the part of a
deep pocket. The burnous may also be shortened by hitching it
up under the arms, or the corners, knotted together, are slipped up
to the chin, or arranged to come at the back of the neck. Indeed,
it is twisted about according to fancy and convenience. The
Kabyles have one dodge for tucking it up when ploughing;
another for making it into a sort of sack to carry forage. When
it is hot they wear it one way; another when it is cold. As
it is impossible to follow these arrangements by simply watching
the people, I got a Kabyle to come for an afternoon and give me
a regular lesson. I took notes, twisted a burnous about my person
in every conceivable fashion, and felt much impressed with the
knottiness of the subject.

The dress of the women is simpler than that of the men; and
being adjusted to the wearer's person in a definite manner, it is,
luckily for comprehension, not so confusing as the burnous.

These dresses are called Aabans, and are strong and warm.
Some are plain, others have ornamental borders, or broad bands of
divers colours worked in geometric patterns; others again are
covered all over with such patterns; some are red, some an indigo
blue.

Their character and style are of great antiquity, yet no two are
quite alike; the individual workwoman, while following a tradition,
reserves liberty for her own ingenuity and taste.

Before long these serviceable and interesting dresses will have
disappeared, and the unfortunate women will then feel the improv-
ing effects of modern civilisation, by having nothing to wear but
villanous coloured pocket-handkerchiefs, and chilly white cotton

goods. Yes, alas! from the draperies of antiquity to dresses of Manchester printed stuff, intended to be cut into handkerchiefs, is a too easy and inevitable jump.

The dress, hanging very loosely about the arms, which are bare for convenience, is sometimes kept closer to the figure, by a red band which passes in a loop over each shoulder, and crosses at the back, where it is ornamented with little red tassels. This is called an Asfifi, and is a pretty feature. When the arms are raised, the loose drapery hanging through the loops has much the appearance of the full sleeve of the Italian peasant.

The Asfifi is interesting as explaining the origin of the corset of the Moorish women, which at the back is only three or four inches in depth; this is merely an Asfifi solidified. The tiny Moorish corset, but little enlarged, was to be found in the old costume of Capri, Procida, and Ischia, in which the corset only reached about half way to the waist.

Shoulder-pins, called Ifizimen, are made of silver, often enriched with coral and enamels, the fastening is just an Irish brooch; they have in addition, triangular ornamented plates of metal attached to the lower end of the fastening. These pins are sometimes connected with a chain, to the centre of which is suspended a little metal box, enamelled, and containing scent.

The girdle, which is called an Argooz, effective in appearance, consists of a quantity of woollen plaits, the prevailing hue red, bound together at points about eighteen inches apart, with cross bindings of bright colours. These ties are sometimes of silk, and the girdles are from fifteen to twenty feet in length.

On the head is worn a little peaked bonnet, like the French cap

of liberty. This is called a Timhárent. It is made by doubling
in half, lengthway, a broad silk band, and sewing up one side. It
is kept in its place by a second kerchief, bound round, and knotted
behind. These silk Timhárents come from Tunis. Many women
allow their hair to wave free, or confine it simply with a fillet.

A frequent ornament is a round silver brooch called a 'Táfizimth,' with an opening in the centre crossed by a pin. Bosses of
coral, as well as knobs of silver, which latter have a very pearl-like
effect, are dotted about it. These are effective pieces of jewellery,
and with the sun shining on them, they glisten like moons. They
are not adopted till a woman becomes a mother. On the birth of
a girl the Táfizimth is worn between the breasts; on the birth of
a boy, it is raised, and gleams above the forehead. Remarking
that many of these brooches offered for sale, were damaged, a
Kabyle gave a frank explanation which was : 'When a man's
wife was disobedient, and got beaten, her custom was to undo the
" Táfizimth " and dash it to the ground at his feet.'

There is another head-ornament, handsomer than this. It is
called a 'Taasubth,' and consists of a central silver brooch over
the forehead, and side brooches above the temples, enriched in the
same style, and with rows of silver gleaming semispheres com-
pletely encircling the head, and forms a glittering tiara fit for a
princess. The ' repoussé ' semispheres are about three-quarters of
an inch in diameter. I have seen this same ornament in Pompeian
jewellery.

Bracelets of ' repoussé ' work, and sometimes silver anklets, are
worn. Necklaces are made of beads and coral, and also of cloves
and sweet-smelling paste, but a handsomer and more characteristic

sort, called a ' Theslegth,' is a row of square silver boxes, containing scents, strung together with pieces of coral.

During the wet weather, I had plenty of time to study my
Kabyle Dictionary and Grammar ; the school children also came
and gave help in learning the language ; and as Kabyles sat in the
tent nearly all day, I had constant opportunities for trying to
speak it, and made progress. Our friends brought a servant
rejoicing in the name of Zachariah, who spoke Arabic ; this was of
service, and we called upon him for help, when mutual ignorance
brought conversation to a dead-lock, as it often did. The Kabyles
are such travellers that in every village some speak Arabic ; but
there is not a woman in the country who understands anything but
Kabyle.

Zachariah was of a cheerful disposition, and made company
for the melancholy Dominique, who however did not grow more
lively in consequence. The latter used to lecture Zachariah, and
give him the advantages of his experience, describe mysterious
and savoury dishes that he had concocted in cities, and recount
the perils to be endured by colonists living amongst Arabs in the
interior. His chief complaint against Zachariah was, ' Ce pauvre
jeune homme ne sait pas beaucoup, cependant il ne demande pas
de conseil.' Those were trying days for both men, when they had
to cook in the pouring rain. Dominique also was extremely
disgusted at the freedom with which we let natives sit in the
entrance to our tent ; he periodically rushed in a perfect frenzy of
rage, at the boys who chaffed him, and ' Dominique Marboul '
(Mad Dominique) became a familiar expression in our ears.

One morning some Kabyles brought two very young boars to

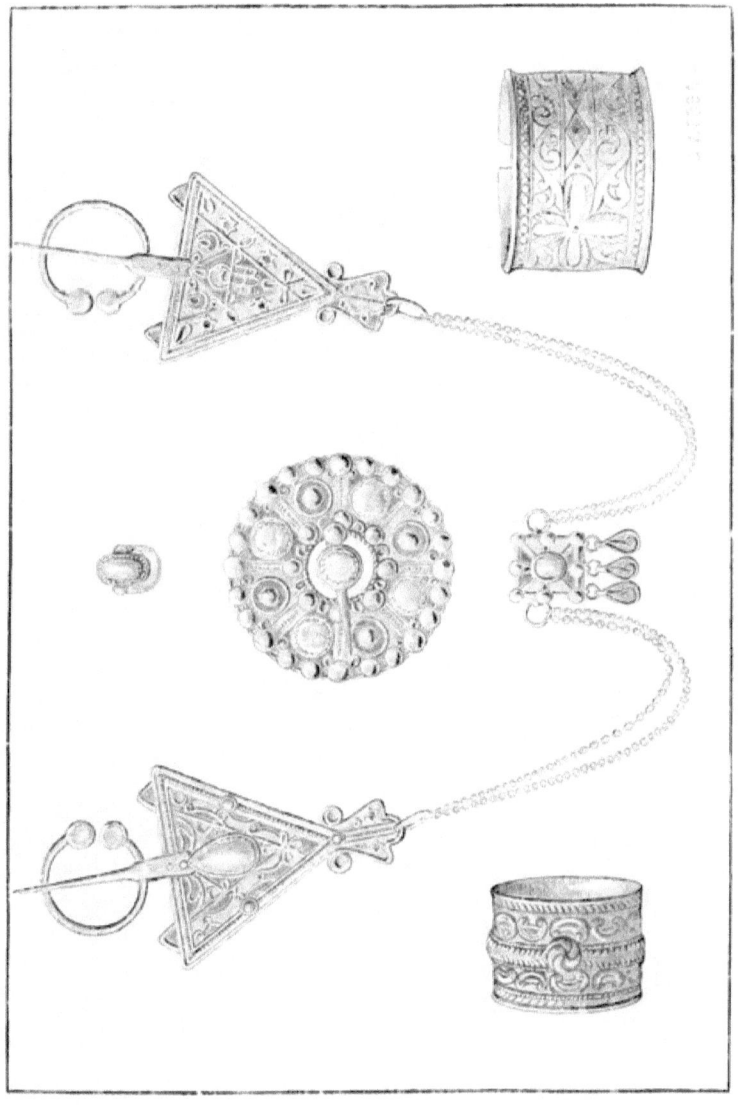

JEWELLERY.

the tents, little brown and yellow striped creatures. Zachariah, taking a fancy to these genuine 'cochons sauvages,' bought them for pets. Little boars, as they grow up, are said to become much attached to their masters, nothing delighting them more than to follow their benefactors incessantly, and by rubbing against their legs, demonstrate their gratitude and affection. One of these dear creatures was put out to nurse, given into the charge of a Kabyle lad to rear, Zachariah undertaking to look after the other himself. Part of our tent was partitioned off into a room for Dominique. Zachariah slept there also; and he hid away his pet in the corner, while Dominique sat opposite, predicting evil for it. The pig had naturally no intention of remaining in one particular spot; and on finding itself alone, went squeaking all about the place, feebly enough, for it was weak and soon grew weaker. On the second day it was 'in extremis,' with a pinched-up look about the body. Zachariah, anxious about the brother out at nurse, had it brought back and set by the fire for warmth. He was called away, and meanwhile the little beast, shivering, toppled into the glowing embers and was roasted. This tragedy was quickly followed by the death of the surviving pig. During the night, while nursed in Zachariah's bosom, with a few faint squeaks, it closed its brief and chastened existence.

Tuesday, May 4, 1880.—H. M.'s leave of absence drew towards a close. He and his comrade could no longer remain, and we were obliged to part with their pleasant company. The mules were laden, and we bade our friends 'bon voyage.'

The trees were now in fulness of summer leaf, but in spite of

I

the rich and rapid growth of all vegetation, owing to the wet, there was not that delicate brilliance which the opening burst of spring presented.

It was just a month since we left Algiers, and we had completed so little, that feelings of despair came upon us.

HEWING.

'Tis more by art, than force of numerous strokes,
The dexterous woodman shapes the stubborn oaks.

POPE's Iliad, Book xxiii.

CHAPTER IV.

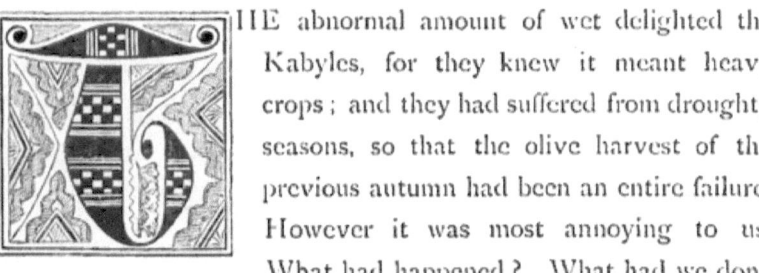

THE abnormal amount of wet delighted the Kabyles, for they knew it meant heavy crops ; and they had suffered from droughty seasons, so that the olive harvest of the previous autumn had been an entire failure. However it was most annoying to us. What had happened ? What had we done to deserve this ? We began to consider the advisability of making some offering to Uncle Zaïd's Kouba, to propitiate the gods.

For Jove his fury pours,
And earth is laden with incessant showers,
When guilty mortals break th' eternal laws,
Or judges, bribed, betray the righteous cause ;
From their deep beds he bids the rivers rise,
And opens all the floodgates of the skies :
Th' impetuous torrents from their hills obey,
Whole fields are drowned, and mountains swept away ;
Loud roars the deluge till it meets the main,
And trembling man sees all his labour vain.

Weather permitting we painted, and as our days much repeated each other, I shall not attempt to follow them regularly, but make desultory remarks upon such things as struck me. One day we went to a neighbouring market, Souk-es-Sebt ; Saturday's market. Unlike Souk-el-Jemãa, this is held at the top of a bare mountain. In clear weather this point must command a magnificent view ; it was very fine with the Jurjura wreathed in clouds. I have given an illustration of men at a market selling fig-cuttings.

> Some in deep mould
> Plant cloven stakes, and (wondrous to behold !)
> Their sharpened ends in earth their footing place,
> And the dry poles produce a living race.

These fig-cuttings look like unpromising bundles of dry sticks ; but 'as the earth bringeth forth her bud, and as the garden causeth the things that are sown in it to spring forth,' even so may the people 'put on the garment of praise for the spirit of heaviness.'

Not till we arrived at the market did we perceive the reason for its being held at such an inconvenient and exposed spot ; we then saw a number of villages before us, perched on the crests of precipitous ridges.

The market is on the boundary between the Aïth Ménguellath and a tribe called the Aïth or Beni Yahïa. Beni is the Arabic for 'sons of,' the word Aït or Aïth has the same meaning in Kabyle. The locality of markets is often on the boundary of tribal territories, such as Souk-es-Sebt and Souk-el-Jemãa. Souk-el-Arba at Fort National, on the contrary, is in the centre of the tribe Beni Iraten.

Such points of junction were esteemed neutral in old days, when the country was disturbed, and tribesmen could attend and transact business in safety when it would have been dangerous to overstep the limits of their own lands.

An institution that rendered travelling in safety possible when the country was embroiled, is that called Anaya, which is a reciprocal compact between two persons to guard each other from attack. A traveller wishing to pass through antagonistic tribes, or for any reason apprehending danger, sought a friend, who granted him Anaya; this friend, if he did not accompany him gave some token, to be presented in the tribe whither the stranger was going, which would ensure the respect and hospitality due to himself; the new host would in his turn offer the stranger Anaya, and so pass him on in safety. Since the French have introduced settled government, this custom has disappeared, or more truly speaking, lies dormant, for I have myself met a Frenchman who assured me that his life was saved by it in 1870. When the revolt broke out, he was far away from home, but a native friend accorded him Anaya, and by means of tokens, he was passed in safety to a French settlement, though the country was in a flame.

A woman could give Anaya in the absence of her husband; it was in consequence of its violation, that a war occurred in which several tribes took part. It was 'à propos' of this same affair, that the villages beneath which we were encamped received the names of 'Taourirt en Taïdith' (The Peak of the Dog) and 'Ouarzen' (the Ogre). The following is the story: A man of the Aïth Bou Yousef, desiring to pass through the territory of the Aïth Mén-guellath, but fearing to fall a victim to the vengeance of an enemy,

presented himself at a house in Taourirt, and solicited Anaya.
His friend being absent, the wife gave him as token a dog, well
known about there as belonging to her husband. Shortly after,
the woman saw her dog return alone, covered with blood. Not
knowing what to think, she called friends together, who starting
in quest of the stranger, soon discovered his body disfigured with
wounds, lying at the bottom of a ravine. Indignation was felt at
this perfidious act ; two parties were formed, and no terms of accommodation being arrived at, fighting began.

The French first dominated this part of the country by march-
ing a column to Souk-es-Sebt, in 1854. The Aïth Ménguellath
finding themselves threatened, tendered submission ; three years
later, in conjunction with other tribes, they rose in arms. They
were then attacked by General Macmahon, who carried their
villages by storm, and consigned them as a prey to the flames.

The tribe of the Beni Yahïa was in former days the nucleus
of a Kabyle state known to Spanish writers as Cuco, which was
also the name of their chief town. It corresponds with the confederation of the Zouáoua. The outlet of the country was by the
roadstead of Azefoun, where commerce was transacted with the
Marseillese. Marmol, who wrote A.D. 1573, gives an account of
the country which answers to its present condition; and he speaks
of the warlike inhabitants, who recognised no master, and paid
tribute to none. They were rich in corn, in flocks, and horses,
and though constantly fighting, they had free markets on neutral
ground, where hostile tribes could do business without fear.

History does not deign to speak much about the Kabyles.
These mountaineers appear to have remained generally untouched

by the political movements that distracted North Africa. A little
book by A. Berbrugger, 'Les Époques Militaires de la Grande
Kabylie,' published 1857, enters into details of their history, though
the author has difficulty to find continuous firm ground for his
statements. What he makes evident is, the unchanging character
of the people, their troublesome and dangerous qualities as neighbours, and the pertinacity with which they were always ready to
fight for their independence.

Ebn Khaldoun, himself a Berber, and the historian of the race,
wrote towards the end of the fourteenth century. He speaks of the
confederation of the Zouáoua, and gives the names of tribes, many
of which still exist. It is to the Zouáoua that the word Zouave
owes its origin. The Kabyles were then less exclusively confined
to the mountains, and many led a nomadic life in the adjoining
plains. They were dressed in striped garments, one end of
which thrown over the shoulder, floated behind, they also had
heavy burnouses, black, and of a tawny brown colour, and went
generally bareheaded, only shaving from time to time.

One day, in the Aïth Ménguellath, I met an old man with a
burnous striped all over with thin dark lines of blue, and further
ornamented with chess-board patterns; this I bought off his back,
as it was the only thing of the sort I had seen in the country. As
the ends of the burnous are commonly flung over the shoulder, I
conclude that the striped garments mentioned by Ibn Khaldoun
were of this nature; though possibly he refers to striped cloths
such as are still worn by the women.

Throughout the long dominion of the Romans, the Berbers
were continually breaking the peace, and were rather hemmed in,

and overawed, than assimilated to the higher civilisation surrounding them.

In those times they were known under the name of the Quinquegentians, or five tribes, and various proofs can be brought to show that they were of a very refractory character. For instance a Roman inscription preserved at Aumale, runs to this effect : ' To Q. Gargilius, victim of the attacks of the Bavars, on account of the love he bore the citizens, and his single-minded affection for his country, and besides, on account of his courage and vigilance in taking and killing the rebel Faraxen with his partisans, the municipal body of Auzia, at its own cost, has raised and dedicated this monument, 24 March 221 of the province.' Or 261 A.D.

The word Faraxen is supposed to apply to the leader of the Beni Fraousen, one of the present principal tribes.

The war of Firmus, an account of which is given by Gibbon, took place in these regions. An outline of the revolt in a few words, is this : The Roman governor of Africa, Count Romanus, instead of protecting the colonists against the inroads of the tribes, sought only by unjust oppressive measures to benefit his own pocket, and having powerful friends at court, he was able to hide his iniquitous proceedings from the Emperor. At this time Nubal was chief of the Zouáoua. He had many sons, some natural, some legitimate. Zammer, a natural son and friend of the governor, was killed in a dispute by a legitimate son, Firmus. He, in order to avoid threatened punishment, revolted, and the rising became formidable on account of the disordered state of the province. This was about A.D. 370. To quell the rebellion, Count Theodosius was sent over to Africa, he landed at the modern Gigelli, and proceeded to Setif, and shortly advanced with an army to Tri-busuptus, the present Bordj Tiklat, some twenty miles from Bougie, where Roman ruins exist in abundance. From this point he proceeded to attack the Quinquegentians. The names of the tribes mentioned are the Tindenses, Massinissenses, Isaflenses, Jubaleni, and Jesaleni. The Massinissenses are still to be recog-nised under the name of the Imsissen; Massen Issa, meaning the sons of Aïssa; the Isaflenses are the Iflissen; the Jubaleni appear to be the mountaineers of the Jurjura, for the Romans were checked in their attack on them, on account of the difficult nature of the country.[1]

The war, after continuing for some time, was brought to a close by the Kabyle chief Firmus destroying himself, to avoid being given up by Igmazen, the chief of the Isaflenses, to the vic-torious Romans. The principal interest of the story of the war is, that it shows the possibility of tracing certain tribes up to

[1] According to Baron H. Aucapitaine the Jubaleni are the moderns Igáouáouen con-cerning whom a neighbouring tribe sings as follows :—

> 'O God, give us snow ! May the sky be full of flakes,
> That the accursed pass may be blocked
> Between us and the Igáouáouen
> Their friendship is a grief,
> Their acquaintance a path with a steep declivity.'

Jubaleni at first recalls the Arabic ' Jibel ' (a mountain). The Arabs however did not appear in the country till many centuries later, and the word Jubaleni has a very ancient and interesting origin. Iolaus, Jolaus, or Jubal was worshipped by the Phœnicians as a god. ' Without doubt he is the Juba or Jubal also worshipped by the Moors. It again occurs in the name of the Mauretanian King Juba, and in the African Jubaltiana. Thus also Iolaus has been retained in the name of the town Iol or Jol.' The word also occurs as an attribute of the god Baal ' Ju-Baal ' (the glory of the Lord.) (See Mövers, *Die Phœni-cier.*) Upon the city of Iol was built the Roman town of Cæsarea, the remains of which are to be seen at Cherchel. According to Mövers, Baal became the national god of the Mauretanians.

this remote period; it proves also to what an extent they were independent, and on what turbulent terms they lived with their neighbours; a state of things which continued till they were conquered by the French.

The Romans on going to North Africa, found native Berber kingdoms, Numidia, Mauretania, Gætulia, Lybia. The inhabitants of these kingdoms were all of one race, and spoke dialects of the same language, usually known as Berber, but the native name for it is Tamazirght or Amazirgh.

In all the more inaccessible places of North Africa their direct descendants are to be found; they speak varieties of the old language, and have the same character and institutions.[1]

Berber belongs to a class of languages named Hamitic, which comprises ancient Egyptian, Coptic, and Ethiopian languages. An obvious peculiarity which strikes an Englishman, is the prevalence of Th sounds, both hard and soft, as in the English words 'the' and 'thin.' T is often softened into Th, and S into Z. But natives of the same village do not always pronounce words alike. For instance, one would say Aït Ménguellat, another the Aïth Ménguellath. Other peculiarities there are, upon which I need hardly enter.

Those who have not tried the experiment, can hardly be aware of the difficulty of writing down the speech of an illiterate peasant, in which sounds recur which do not exist in European language. It would require an intimate knowledge of the various sections of the Berber race, to have a just appreciation of their language,

---

[1] The inhabitants of the Canary Islands, if not originally of Berber race, have at any rate been subject to Berber dominion at a time anterior to their discovery by Europeans (see Hyde-Clarke, *Ethnological Society*).

classified as Morocco Berber, called Shilha, or Tamazirght, descended from ancient Mauretanian; Berber of the Jurjura and Aures mountains, or Kabyle, descended from ancient Numidian; Touareg from ancient Gætulian; and Ghadames from ancient Garamantian.

The number of localities in Kabylia where traces of the Romans have been found, are too numerous to mention. On the coast were the towns of Saldæ, the modern Bougie; Rusuccurum, now Dellys; and Rusazus, now Azeffoun. There are ruins of importance at Taksebt on Cape Tedles, and at Jemāa-es-Sahridj, a central point in the tribe of the Beni Fraousen. This latter spot I visited in 1873. Its site is beautiful, and celebrated for abundance of springs. I have a pleasant recollection of the songs of nightingales among shady groves, and of the courteous manners of the rural chief, who was entertaining his friends beneath a cane-trellised arbour; but I cannot say I was much impressed by the antiquities, which consist chiefly of rubble walls on the top of a hill. In the market-place are blocks of masonry, supposed to be the remains of a Roman bath. It is obvious to the most uninitiated in military matters, that a station here must have blocked the natural outlet from the higher mountains towards the sea. Since my visit, a flourishing school has sprung up under the superintendence of the Jesuits.

The Kabyles, engaged in internal disputes and struggles to maintain their independence, having their simple wants satisfied by rude manufactures and the land they tilled, never had intercourse with nations more advanced than themselves, and felt not their own deficiencies. Every man guarded above all things his individual

liberty, with a jealousy that prevented him combining with others
to carry out any works of importance, and none had the capital
which might have induced the many to labour for an end in common ; the only sentiment of sufficient strength to bind them
together was fear of the invader. From time immemorial Kabylia
has been the home of peasant proprietorship, of communism, of
local self-government with popular assemblies, of social equality ;
but owing to the limited resources of the country, to the crude
notion that the people have of liberty, and to an excess of the
democratic spirit, their civilisation has crystallised in a primitive
form.

The French have now changed all this, and hold the country
with a firm hand. But in 1870 they were obliged to withdraw
from Algeria most of their troops in order to fight the Germans.

Incited by ill-judging men, the native tribes unhappily thought
the moment to strike for independence had come ; they rose, and
committed barbarous and frightful excesses ; though, to be just
towards them, the cruelties they had themselves suffered from
must be borne in mind. The Franco-German war over, the troops
returned and put down the revolt. The French, full of the bitterest
feelings, confiscated the rich wheat-growing lands, and imposed a
crushing war tribute, that it took the Kabyles five years to pay.
Complete disarmament was also effected, and the country became
for the first time safe. Fort Napoleon sustained a long siege
without being the worse for it, and changed its name to Fort
National, with this new era of ' Liberté, Égalité, et Fraternité.'

It was defended by native troops, who thus proved their fidelity
under the most painful circumstances. Great numbers of Kabyles

have been ruined, and forced to gain their bread by working for the French, and many disgusted with the state of things, have fled to enjoy the license of the native province of Tunis, in districts remote from the hated foreigner.[1]

A knowledge of French is essential for natives who desire to gain a livelihood by working for Europeans, and likewise in the settlement of disputes, which otherwise are fostered by go-betweens, who thrive on the ignorant by pretending to advance their interests with those who govern. It is specially to this work of education that the missionary Fathers apply themselves. They

[1] Since writing the above, the French have entered Tunis, and at the point of the bayonet, have forced the Bey to sign a treaty. In future there is to be progress, and we have the gratification of learning that already civilisation is advancing in its normal manner. In the 'Daily News' of June 7, was a letter from the correspondent in the French camp, dated May 26, 1881, in which he gives an interesting account of the introduction of the old Algerian institution of razzia into Tunis, which he thus graphically describes. 'It is simple in its aim, simple in its execution. It requires but one condition : You must be stronger than the enemy or friend towards whom the razzia is directed. The receipt is : Take a sufficiently strong force, scour the country of the enemy or friend, drive off all his cattle, if necessary spoil his crops, burn his tents, and if it is possible to perform a good clean sweeping razzia without shooting anybody, do not do so.' 'Depreciation of property is of course the effect of a razzia. The French find themselves with more cattle than they know what to do with, and sell them to the highest bidder. I have had pointed out to me a Frenchman whose business it is to go from one camp to another picking up cattle cheap. The effect on the Arabs themselves is, they will sell everything they have for what it will fetch, feeling that at any moment it may be taken from them.'

The letter continues, 'I have always made it my business to inquire about the Kroumirs. Here, as elsewhere, I find the same story. Few people have ever seen one.' 'So certain is every one that no further fighting can possibly occur, and that any attempt to find the Kroumirs is abandoned, that I leave for Tunis to-morrow, marvelling much at a campaign that has had no beginning, no middle, no ending, and that has taken 40,000 troops away from their homes to invade the country of an enemy who has been invisible.' The Kroumirs (if they really exist) are Berbers, and there is no reason to believe that they are worse people than those I have described living amongst. Owing to some unknown mental process, the French colonist believes that ingratitude is a fundamental defect in the native character ; and concludes that, on account of this ineradicable moral cancer, he is not beloved and respected as he ought to be.

are a society recognised by the State, on the understanding that they do not interfere with the religion of the people. There is besides, little temptation for them to do so, as the jealousy of the natives would be aroused, and their influence with them consequently lost. Truly it would be foolish to cherish fallacious hopes of converting the Kabyles ; they respect the sincerity of the Fathers, but there are too many nominal Christians in the land, who, the natives remark, do not believe in their own Marabouts.

The Fathers are the only Europeans that the natives think disinterested friends ; the single-minded devotion with which they give themselves to a useful and philanthropic mission, causes them to be universally honoured. An extensive field lies open ; so much so, that one is struck by the disproportion between means and aims ; they are a forlorn hope of Christian knights valiantly assaulting the stronghold of ignorance ; men doing battle on the summit of a scaling ladder, without sympathy given by the army encamped at a distance. Until these schools were founded, the natives picked up French under difficulties. The following translation of a song, will give the reader their sentiments concerning their study of the language :

SONG.

The day on which 'bon soir' was revealed to us,
We received a blow on the jaw.
We were nailed in prison.

The day on which 'bon jour' was revealed to us,
We received a blow on the nose.
Blessings have ceased.

The day on which 'merci' was revealed to us,
We were taken by the throat.
A sheep inspires more fear than we.

The day on which ' cochon' was revealed to us,
A dog had more honour than we.
The farmer has bought a mule.

The day on which 'frère' was revealed to us,
We received a kick on the knee.
We wade in shame up to the breast.

The day on which 'diable' was revealed to us,
We received a blow which made us mad.
We have become porters of dung.

One lovely day, bright and cloudless, on approaching the cemetery of Thililit, we heard the chanting of many voices. There
was a funeral. The corpse, wrapped closely round in a white sheet
and carried on a stretcher, was laid on the ground ; a Kabyle sat
beside and led the chant, while the friends of the dead man, in
picturesque groups, stood round the grave ; one carried a crown
of oleander. The body was lowered, the earth filled in, and flag-
stones fastened down on the top ; there was another chant, and
then the people dispersed. The cattle, sheep, and goats grazed
unconcernedly around ; the pastoral pipe but halted an hour in
its soft-toned warblings. When it recommenced, it might
perchance have mourned the loss of a brother piper, in the fashion
of antique measures :

' The fountain nymphs through the wood mourn for thee, and
their tears become waters ; and echo amid the rocks laments,
because thou art mute, and mimics no more thy lips ; and at thy
death, the trees have cast off their fruit, and the flowers have all
withered ; good milk hath not flowed from ewes, nor honey from
hives, but it has perished in the wax, wasted with grief; for no
longer is it meet, now that thy honey is lost, to gather that.'

The long line of mourners issuing from the cemetery was a beautiful spectacle; golden reflections in shadowed burnouses harmonising charmingly with the lichened tombstones. A youth only remained behind, the son of the deceased; he sat upon the tomb wailing.

I have sometimes seen locks of hair laid upon graves, reminding of similar Greek offerings.

In the play of 'Electra,' Orestes says :—

> first honouring my father's grave,
> As the god bade us, with libations pure and tresses from our brow.

Electra at her father's tomb says to her sister :

> And then do thou,
> Cutting the highest locks that crown thy head,
> Yea, and mine also, poor although I be,
> (Small offering, yet 'tis all the store I have,)
> Give to him ; yes, this lock, untrimmed,
> Unmeet for suppliant's vow.

The first discovered traces of the return of Orestes are offerings laid on their father's tomb.

Chrysosthemis, the younger sister, says :—

> And lo ! my father's bier was crowned
> With garlands of all flowers that deck the fields ;
> And, seeing it, I wondered, and looked round,
> Lest any man should still be hovering near ;
> And when I saw that all the place was calm,
> I went yet nearer to the mound, and there
> I saw upon the topmost point of all
> A tress of hair, fresh severed from the head.

On a previous visit to Kabylia, when living at a farmhouse in part of which resided a native family, I one morning heard a

lamentable cry, and running out, I, unperceived, observed what
passed. A man sat crouched upon a stone, with burnous flung
about him, and hands pressed against his bent-down head; his
attitude was precisely that of mourning figures I have seen painted
on Greek vases.

At his side stood a woman swaying backwards and forwards,
with face raised as if questioning that stainless sky which
seemed to mock her with its deep serenity, with wearisome
iteration uttering the same piteous lament. She held her arms
stretched upwards, and ever and anon her clenched fists descended
with merciless blows upon her breasts. A boy, their first-born,
had just fallen down dead in a fit. The parents rushed out of
the house into the fields, and in this unaffected manner they
showed their anguish. The image of that poor woman will ever
remain graven in my memory, a picture of dire and bitter
lamentation. What passionate gestures were these! How
human! But how un-English! This vehemence, this spreading
forth of hands when there was none to comfort, recalled Biblical
wailings.

' Behold, I cry out of wrong, but I am not heard: I cry aloud,
but there is no judgment. He hath fenced up my way that I cannot pass, and he hath set darkness in my paths. He hath stripped
me of my glory, and taken the crown from my head. He hath
destroyed me on every side, and I am gone: and my hope hath he
removed like a tree.'

The day after the funeral at Thililit, we returned to the same
place and found two big vultures promenading slowly backwards
and forwards over the fresh grave; they remained there the

L

greater part of the afternoon. What mysterious faculties have these birds, both of wing and scent. At Souk-el-Jemãa, we saw a flock of thirty or forty, sitting on the refuse of the slaughtered animals, whilst the market was still crowded, and we approached within twenty paces without disturbing their repast. There must be a great number in the high mountains, for some are usually in sight. When painting, I have heard a rushing noise overhead, have looked up, and seen one of these great birds sweeping swiftly along without moving a feather. Thus they wing their flight, soaring in any direction to a prodigious distance, performing this feat apparently by a mere effort of the will. The power this bird possesses of discovering its prey is attributed in the Book of Job to keenness of vision.

'There is a path which no fowl knoweth, and which the vulture's eye hath not seen.'

'Whence then cometh wisdom? and where is the place of understanding? Seeing it is hid from the eyes of all living, and kept close from the fowls of the air.'

Eagles also are common, some of great size.

One day last winter an eagle pounced on a chicken that was unconcernedly pecking about in front of a cottage in Taourirt Amokran. For an instant the bird remained half stunned by its rapid descent, and a Kabyle sitting in the doorway, threw his burnous and caught it alive. They are not birds to be trifled with, and I was told how, on another occasion, a Kabyle following a badly wounded eagle, was attacked by the bird, which struck at his head, clawed out one of his eyes, and would have killed him, had not a friend come to his assistance. Neither of us had provided ourselves with guns, and our encampment would not have been well chosen for sport. The natives kill a few wild boars in the ravines, hares, partridges and quail; it was the closed season, but they bagged partridges nevertheless, going out with a call-bird to attract others. Quails are left almost unmolested on account of their nests being in the midst of the ripening corn. We continually heard their liquid note of contentment, for contented they no doubt were, living unharassed in the midst of such abundance.

A sportsman brought some birds of fine plumage, which I skinned; but having only salt to cure them with, the ants got at them, and few remained of any value.

The hoopoo is common; we often heard its thrice-repeated flute-like note, or saw it with crest proudly erect, perched on the top-most branch of a tree. A young one was brought us which we thought of rearing, an odd little bird, always looking as if going to topple over; it had no tail, and the crest and long bill looked out of all proportion; it perhaps resented being laughed at, for it had a furious temper, which we knew not how to conciliate; and when the little creature was discovered one morning to be missing, it was not followed by many regrets. The golden oriole is not un-common. Other birds more familiar were not wanting; fre-quently we heard the home-reminding notes of the cuckoo; and swallows flitted about all day. At dinner-time they would perch on a figtree within six feet of us, gently chatter, skim through the air, and return to chatter again.

Of butterflies I noticed none that are not native to England; but I found a curious insect, simulating exactly a decaying leaf of evergreen oak ; under the microscope it has the appearance of being covered with crystallised spikes.

When it became hot, ants were busy in every direction ; one sort, with a big red head half as large again as its black body, was remarkable for long legs, it ran more quickly that any other ant I ever saw ; there were lots of these always in a hurry. I noticed one enter a nest of small black ants, and afterwards reappear without commotion ensuing ; probably a hot-headed freak of curiosity. If I were to bolt into the houses of the Kabyles in that manner, thought I, I should meet with a very different reception.

Several times I saw swarms of wild bees. I have seen the boys, who were quick in detecting the approaching hum, spring to their feet and rush off in wild excitement, I knew not at first why. They tried to change the course of the swarm by throwing dust into the air ; it was a pretty sight—eager boys with draperies tossed and flying about, and an afternoon sun lighting up the handfuls of dust and the swarming bees.

> Thus in the season of unclouded spring,
> To war they follow their undaunted king,
> Crowd through their gates, and in the fields of light
> The shocking squadrons meet in mortal fight.
> . . . . this deadly fray
> A cast of scatter'd dust will soon allay,
> And undecided leave the fortunes of the day.

On this occasion the scattered dust had no effect, for the winged army poured on.

> Dusky they spread a close-embodied crowd,
> And o'er the vale descends the living cloud.

Another evening, two lads returning home with our painting

traps suddenly put down their loads. One of them, Kassi, troubled with great animal spirits, always up to mischief, made passes with a stick at a bush by the wayside, protecting himself by throwing his burnous about his head. We found him in great excitement, thrusting at a wasp's nest hanging in the bush. It reminded me of another of Homer's similes in the 'Iliad.'

> As wasps, provok'd by children in their play,
> Pour from their mansions by the broad highway,
> In swarms the guiltless traveller engage,
> Whet all their stings, and call forth all their rage ;
> All rise in arms, and with a gen'ral cry
> Assert their waxen domes, and buzzing progeny.

In this case the guiltless travellers remained unstung, and Kassi was called off before he learnt that the wasps could fight like Greeks ; for Homer says again :

> When wasps from hollow crannies drive
> To guard the entrance of their common hive,
> Dark'ning the rock, while with unweary'd wings
> They strike th' assailants, and infix their stings.
> A race determined that to death contend,
> So fierce these Greeks their last retreats defend.

And again—

> So burns the vengeful hornet (soul all o'er),
> Repuls'd in vain, and thirsty still of gore ;
> Bold son of air and heat, on angry wings
> Untam'd, untir'd, he turns, attacks, and stings.

Formidable wild animals are rare, but are still to be found in fastnesses where wild boar offer means of subsistence ; they are occasionally driven abroad from their lairs into populated parts, by winter's severity. Then the unhorned tenants of the wood, sorely grinding their teeth, roam the thickets ; 'then truly are they like unto a man that goes on a stick, whose back is well-nigh broken, and head looks towards the ground ; like such an one they roam, shunning the white snow.'

Last winter there was an unusually heavy fall of snow, covering Kabylia with a coat more than a foot thick ; it still whitened all northern slopes and blocked the passes, when I visited the country six weeks later. I was told that the roar of a lion had been heard shortly before, in a ravine of the Aïth Ménguellath ; this may possibly be true : the Fathers told us that they heard the laugh of the hyena.

Returning last winter to Algiers, whilst passing through the village of Tizi-Ouzou, a dead panther was brought in, shot by a native beside a stream ten miles off, in a populous district separated from the Jurjura by a broad valley ; and a little later a second was killed in the same neighbourhood. Curiously, when I was at Tizi-Ouzou before, the same incident occurred ; the panther had then been shot in the forests in the direction of Bougie. The only wild animals we came across while camping were jackals, which are numerous ; on fine nights we heard their wild empty-stomached howls, when they prowled up from the valleys, and all the dogs in the villages would begin barking. These were the only discordant noises at night ; more pleasant was the constant sound of distant frogs croaking in damp places, the welcome melody of nightingales, and the melancholy note of a bird called the Taab, which I believe to be some kind of owl.

And owls that mark the setting sun, declare
A star-light evening and a morning fair.

That solitary mysterious note, hardly uttered before answered in another quarter by some brother, suggested how, when rude settlements dreaded night attacks, the owl, harmless towards men, might from its sleepless vigilance have been chosen to symbolise a protecting goddess of wisdom.

We heard also little animals pattering over the tent in the dark, sometimes rustling the papers under our beds. Thinking of field-mice as likely to make these sounds, we sent for a trap; we caught a few only, and ultimately discovered that the noise was caused by harmless green lizards. I was not aware that these creatures run about in the dark; they must have singular eyes, for animals that are active by night do not usually dart about in the brilliancy and heat of noonday.

May 21 to *June* 14, 1880.—The wet season came at last to a close, and we were favoured with the most perfect weather imaginable. The heat was by no means oppressive, and the air was bracing and life-giving, the sky was of exquisite colour, and the light so intense that the tops of the trees seemed frosted with silvery flashing lights. All snow had disappeared from the high mountains, except here and there a minute patch; a pale apple-green played on their slopes mixed with delicate rosy grey tones, a mass of subtle glowing tints softened by the purple bloom of distance. The azure of the sky appeared to soak into the landscape and blend with the flesh-tint of the distant soil. Fallow fields, as if stirred by a secret spirit of joy they could no longer restrain, brought forth a multitude of wild flowers, whilst the corn turned by degrees from green to gold. The natives changed their hours for going a-field, becoming more matinal. On the first signs of approaching dawn, the birds broke out in a concert of melody ; this was followed by the pleasant chattering of the women going to draw water. When the sun rose and 'tipped the hills with gold,' the men appeared with their flocks.

> Haste, to the stream direct thy way,
> When the gay morn unveils her smiling ray ;
> Haste to the stream !

Between ten and eleven they drove them home again ; then they dined and reposed themselves, while the beasts were kept in the cool. After three o'clock men were again abroad, till deepening twilight ushered in the night, when lanes were crowded with flocks, herds, and tired peasants slowly mounting homewards. Except during these hours we saw few people, and felt at last like mariners stranded on a forsaken shore. This was because most of the male population betook themselves to the plains about Algiers and Constantine in quest of employment, as it was a time of year when extra hands were required for harvesting ; on their return with a small store of hardly-earned money, as soon as the harvest of their own fields has been garnered, then is the season for feasts and marriages.

The effects at sunset were magical : the mountains would turn to warm violet and gold, set off by the greens and purples of nearer ranges. The sky was of a mellow Claude-like serenity, and as the sun sank rocks and trees glowed with a more than Venetian warmth of colour. It was curious to observe how differently trees took the light. Ash seemed to grow greener, whilst ilexes and corks lost their green altogether and appeared of a rich glowing bronze. We were not without good intentions of trying to represent this ; but whenever the looked-for moment came, and splendours deepened about us, we put aside brushes with feelings of despair.

At this hour there was no fear of chill or fever, for the warm air in the confined valleys rose gradually.

Among the studies we painted in these days was one of the fountain ; we had anticipated remonstrance, but none was made.

One day a party of men begged us not to go painting there, as a ceremony was about to be held, nor were the women allowed to draw water after their early morning visit. At mid-day sheep were slaughtered and cut up under the shade of the trees, the meat carried to the villages, and the greater part, I understood, was given away to the poor. The richer men had contributed the animals ; the chief Marabout also assisted at the slaughter. After this some slight repairs were effected, stones that formed a rude paving in front of the fountain were relaid, and weeds growing too luxuriantly were pulled up.

I did not hear of this custom in other tribes, and I could not understand what ideas they associated with it. It must not be confounded with the great Mahommedan festival that occurs later, when there is a general slaughtering of sheep, so that everyone can eat mutton. It looks like a relic of Pagan sacrifice, which may well be, in a country so unchanging. Have not the women from time immemorial carried their pitchers to the fountains just as they do now ? An early Greek vase in the British Museum represents women carrying vases in the same way I saw here. When the pitcher is empty and more difficult to balance, it is laid on its side

upon a kerchief wound into a circle and placed on the head ; the
mouth of the vase projects in front ; one handle kept lower than
the other rests on the edge of the twisted kerchief, and helps to
steady the vase ; an arm raised to it is therefore bent.   When the
vase is filled and poised on the head, both handles are at a convenient height to be grasped when the arms are at full stretch.

The most interesting relic of ancient custom that I have met
with in the country, was at a marriage festival at Aïn Soltān in
the neighbourhood of Borj Boghni.

The bridegroom had gone to fetch his bride, and I waited with
many others beside a stream that passed at the foot of the village,
for his return.   Suddenly we heard the sound of pipes, and saw the
marriage procession streaming from the summit of a neighbouring
hill, and then lose itself among the trees ; a few minutes later it
issued from an avenue near us, and ascended a slope towards the
bridegroom's house.   First came the pipers, then the bride muffled
up in a veil, riding a mule led by her lover.   As well as I could
judge, she was very young, almost a child.   Then came a bevy of
gorgeously dressed damsels, sparkling with silver ornaments,
followed by a crowd of other friends, and Kabyle Dick and Harry.
In front of the bridegroom's house the procession stopped ; the
girl's friends lined both sides of the pathway and crowded about
the door.   The pipers marched off on one side, while the bridegroom lifted the girl from the mule and held her in his arms.
The girl's friends thereupon threw earth at him, when he hurried
forward, and carried her over the threshold, those about the door
beating him all the time with olive branches amid much laughter.
This throwing of earth, this mock opposition and good-natured

scourging, appeared to be a symbolised relic of marriage by capture, and was a living explanation of the ancient Roman custom of carrying the bride over the threshold of her lover's house.

In the evening on such occasions the pipers and drummers are called in, and the women dance, two at a time, facing each other ; nor does a couple desist until, panting and exhausted, they step aside to make room for another. The dance has great energy of movement, though the steps are small and changes of position slight, the dancers only circling round occasionally. But they swing their bodies about with an astonishing energy and suppleness. As leaves flutter before the gale, so do they vibrate to the music ; they shake, they shiver and tremble, they extend quivering arms, wave veils, which they sometimes cast over their heads thrown backwards like Bacchantes, and their minds seem lost in the '*abandon*' and frenzy of the dance, while the other women looking on, encourage by their high piercing trilling cries, which add to the noise of the pipes and drums. They also deride the men by clapping their hands to the music and singing verses such as the following :—

> Oh alack ! alack ! Oh dear one, most dear,
> Come now—to the place we have spoken of.
>
> Oh grafted apple ! thy love kills me !
> An old grey head reposes on thy arm.
>
> Oh Thithen ! Thithen ! with the motley-coloured girdle,
> Oh sweet apple ! grafted upon a root.
>
> Beauty to marvel at have the Aïth Ouagóuenoun,
> Their skin is sleek, their eyes are dark.
>
> Oh winged bird ! rest thou near to her upon the figtree,
> When Yamina goes forth, kiss me her little cheek.

Even amidst the pomp and splendour of imperial Rome, marriage festivals must have presented some curious resemblances to such primitive customs as I have described, doubtless owing to unrecorded common causes in the remote past.

The bride was brought home in procession, accompanied by the singing of a song and playing on the flute; she was carried over the threshold, and in the evening there was a marriage feast. This habit of carrying the bride was accounted for in various ways.

'Concerning the bride they do not allow her to step over the threshold of the house, but people sent forward carry her over, perhaps because they in old time seized upon women and compelled them in this manner.'[1]

Another explanation, and I think a far less probable one, is that she thus avoided the chance of tripping at the threshold, which would have been considered an omen of bad fortune. To most people it would appear a sufficiently bad augury if she required help at such a moment to prevent her stumbling. Why should she stumble? 'Carefully raise over the threshold thy feet, O bride! Without tripping begin this path, in order that for thy husband thou mayest always be secure.'

> Let the faithful threshold greet,
> With omens fair, those lovely feet,
>   Lightly lifted o'er ;
> Let the garlands wave and bow
> From the lofty lintel's brow
>   That bedeck the door.
>
> See the couch with crimson dress
> Where, seated in a deep recess,

---

[1] See Becker's 'Gallus.'

With expectation warm,
The bridegroom views her coming near ;
The slender youth that led her here
May now release her arm.

In early times, the marriage banquet was not a mere matter of ceremony. It was desirable to have as many witnesses as possible, and such were the guests. At Greek marriages there was likewise a procession with song and flute accompaniment, a feast in the evening, and songs and dance before the nuptial chamber.

Theocritus in his 'Epithalamium of Helen,' describes the twelve first maidens of the city forming the dance in front of the newly-painted nuptial chamber. 'And they began to sing, I ween, all beating time to one melody with many-twinkling feet, and the house was ringing round with a nuptial hymn.'

It was the custom both in Greece and in Italy, when the marriage procession halted before the bridegroom's house, to salute it with a shower of sweetmeats. This recalls the ruder shower of earth that I saw in Kabylia, and which I took to symbolise a volley of stones. The custom still survives in Italy ; for I have often seen sweetmeats thrown among the crowd when a newly-married couple have issued from church ; great is the delight and eager the scrambling of small boys on such occasions.

CHAPTER V.

E originally proposed to move about the country with the tent, though we had fixed on no particular limit or direction to these imaginary travels. But in the middle of the month of June here were we still in the Aïth Ménguellath, not fifteen miles from Fort National. We had plenty to occupy us at the place where we happened to find ourselves, and we reckoned that moving meant expense and new difficulties with natives, and that we might go farther and fare worse.

It was now too hot to wander. Muirhead being anxious to go to Constantine (which I had visited), we now determined to quit our encampment 'under the greenwood tree,' where we had met with 'no enemy but winter and rough weather,' he proceeding thither, whilst I returned with the tent to Algiers, where we should meet again.

I had foreseen that in such an out-of-the-way place, where the men are so jealous, I could not hope to get women to sit as models, and consequently came armed with a camera and gelatine plates. I now took a number of instantaneous photographs of subjects in motion, that I could hardly have sketched.

The narrow paths favoured me, for the natives were forced to pass the very spot I had previously focused, and got caught 'unbeknown' to themselves. Whether they happened to group well or ill at the instant I had to expose, was of course a chance, but if they did not appear interesting, I postponed my shot. The extreme damp of the tent caused me much anxiety about the plates, but the Indian bullock trunk in which I kept them was sturdy, and though some were spoilt, the majority turned out well. The Kabyles would ask to look into the machine, and I was always glad to show it, but first I blocked the light from the lenses, and with much ado spread the cloth over their heads. All that they then saw was the landscape at their backs reflected as in a mirror. Having regarded the lens as a sort of evil eye pointed at them, they were puzzled when they found that the machine apparently looked out from the back of its head in the opposite direction. I thought it kind on my part to show the images the right way up, and they were always much pleased with the effect.

The moments when figures group together harmoniously are so fleeting, that at the best there is barely time to note the leading arrangement. One combination is followed by another, and then another, and noting each in an imperfect manner, it is impossible to compare them justly. Photography has quite lately come to such perfection, that it is now possible with its aid to seize on those instants of time, and reproduce them with unerring precision ; they can afterwards be studied at leisure. Thus the camera can give new and admirable material for artistic taste and fancy to play upon. I certainly bagged records of passing combinations with as much certainty as a sportsman brings down birds.

At dawn on June 16, I bade Muirhead good-bye, and he started for Constantine. The same day I struck tent, and left for the neighbouring tribe of the Beni Ienni, where I proposed remaining a short time. This point was only a few miles away from my direct line of march.

After some trouble about mules, I started, and an hour's ride down a steep path brought me to the foot of the mountain, where I halted for Dominique who was lagging behind. Here a broad watercourse of grey stones, with diminutive cliffs on each side, was overgrown with oleander, a profuse mass of delicate pink bloom. More beautiful than anything to be found in well-tended gardens, was this wealth of blossom in a spot so lonely; beloved but by the sunshine, unvisited but by wandering Zephyr. Nor were the oleanders alone in their happiness; numberless plants and flowers kept them company. The pepper-tree grew luxuriantly, and was particularly beautiful from its fresh and feathery foliage, and the interesting drawing of its stems. Dominique overtook me, and we proceeded. The ravine where I found myself joined a larger one, through which flowed a brisk stream utilised to irrigate adjoining fields. Besides flowering oleanders were well-cared-for plantations of oranges and pomegranates, the latter ablaze with exquisite flame-red blossoms; and vigorous wild vines, rejoicing in the hot sun, greedy to bear a burden of luscious fruit, half suffocated the more sober trees forced to support them. A plumy carpet of ferns spread about their feet. The wooded sides of the gorge rose abruptly, and brilliant light silvered the olives crowning precipitous heights. These mountain streams that ripple so refreshingly in the summer season, become boiling torrents in the winter time, after heavy rains, or when the newly-fallen snows on the Jurjura melt. Suddenly rising, they cut off all communication between the tribes.

> So some simple swain his cot forsakes,
> And wide thro' fens an unknown journey takes ;
> If chance a swelling brook his passage stay,
> And foam impervious cross the wanderer's way,
> Confus'd he stops, a length of country past,
> Eyes the rough waves, and, tired, returns at last.

It was a hot pull up the mountain, but having got to the top, I followed a path to the school-house of the Jesuit fathers, where a very cordial reception awaited me.

I had been told that there was a likely place for camping near their house. On inspection I found it was shadeless, and so retraced my steps for about a mile, to a piece of public ground I had already noticed, where I set to work to pitch the tent. The situation reminded me of Thililit. This done I called on the Kaïd, who chatted in French of his experiences during a visit to the International Exhibition of 1878, and showed me a workshop attached to his house, where jewellers were busy. On leaving, he sent a young man to get me fuel, a matter about which I had left Dominique anxious. On returning to the tent, I found a party of merry inquisitive schoolboys, whose leader, a bright lad, was the son of the Kaïd, and spoke French fluently ; they accompanied me on a walk.

N

The following morning I began a sketch of the village under which I was encamped, houses peeping picturesquely through foliage. Dominique was in his worst humour; his wages had been paid before leaving the Aïth Ménguellath, and having now some notes sewn up in his coat, and seeing Fort National in the distance, he thought he could do as he liked. I had to explain that I proposed remaining master. The upshot was, that flying into a fury, he picked up that wonderful cardboard box and a cage with a tame blackbird he had amused himself with rearing, and walked off. I watched his receding back with feelings of relief, and then pounced on the breakfast which still simmered on the fire. Afterwards, upon lighting my pipe I considered my awkward situation; for the tent could not be left a moment unguarded. About the end of the third pipe, the young man who had gone for firewood luckily made his appearance; I left the tent in his charge, and went to see the Kaïd again. Explaining my case, I added that I should prefer a native to serve me, if a trustworthy one could be found; he said the Fathers would know of someone; so, after a cup of coffee, he most politely accompanied me to the school-house.

The walk was just in the greatest heat of the day, and I began to fear lest this by no means too solid flesh should thaw entirely away on the road. The Fathers promised to send for a young man, a carpenter, formerly a pupil of theirs, who had cooked for them, and understood French. I supped at the school-house that evening, met and engaged him, and wrote out an agreement, signed one copy, and handed Mohammed another to sign. He hesitated; he had forgotten how to write his name. 'Well, put a cross,' suggested the Father. He did so ; an odd signature for a Mussul-man.

It must always be a pleasure to praise the merits of an old pupil, but sometimes it is an imprudence, I reflected. However, Mohammed turned out gentle, obliging, and faithful, and he cooked sufficiently well for me, though he had not the ideal ' Potages des Petits Menus' of Dominique in his head. He filled up spare time by nicking a stick of wild-olive all over with ingenious patterns. If one should believe M. C. Souvestre, who has published a book entitled ' Instructions Secrètes des Jésuites,' it is a sign of little wisdom to apply to the Society of Jesus for a servant. I read that a certain worthy Père Valeze Reynald considers that, ' Les domestiques peuvent prendre en cachette les biens de leurs maitres par forme de compensation, sous pré-texte que leurs gages sont trop modiques, et ils sont dispensés de la restitution.' With such professors and a despised ' cochon d'indigène' for a pupil, I ought to have obtained something quite diabolical.

Night began to darken, the moon rose in splendour from behind the mountains, and a troop of merry boys walked with me along the narrow path among fields of ripe corn that led to my tent. I found four guards awaiting me, who rolled them-selves up in their burnouses and passed the night as sentinels. I did not think them necessary, and the Kaïd told me that he apprehended no danger, but he was responsible for my safety, and that it was an old custom of the country, dating from before the French conquest, which he thought right to keep up. The guards spoke well of their Kaïd, as a man who kept things up to the

mark ; in their tribe they did things proper, not like the Aïth
Ménguellath, poor creatures, who go on anyhow. The Aïth
Ménguellath had said to me, ' Thou forsakest friends to fall among
thieves in the Beni Ienni.'

To enumerate the settlements of the Beni Ienni contained in
a circle within a radius of a mile, will show how thickly inhabited
is Kabylia.

On the precipitous brow nearest to the Fort is Aït el Hassan,
with a population of 1500 souls. A large cemetery, and a rise on
which the Jesuit school-house is built, separate it from Aït l'Arba,
with a population of 900. A little further is Taourirt Mimoun, a
place of equal size. The ridge again descends to the flat piece of
ground where I was. A quarter of a mile off is Taourirt el
Hadjadj, somewhat smaller. Near Taourirt Mimoun, on a
southern arm, is the fifth village, Agouni Hameth ; a little below is
the sixth, Thisgirth by name.

The nests of the Kabyles, like those of the eagles, are built on
high in healthy mountain air. They are thus exposed fully to all
the vicissitudes of the circling seasons. They first receive the
white mantle that winter spreads, they first feel the gusty puffs of
coming sirocco, and are earliest enveloped in the chill mist that the
north wind sweeps from the Mediterranean. In the brightness of
spring mornings they sparkle in sunshine, while white mists cover
the profound valleys, like the waters of a lake. Later on, the
sun stirs this sea of cloud, and lets through the day ; then
fleecy messengers surround the villages, hastening upwards to sail
in silvery brightness through the sky, bearing afar glad promises
of refreshment and abundance. In summer, when the human bees

have stored their harvest, like honey in a hive, then the little
houses seem clustered together, that each may give kindly shade
to its neighbour, scorched in the burning sunshine.

Thus the people live not estranged from nature, like men in
cities, but from lofty outlooks are constant spectators of the
wonders she works, and the beauty in which she delights.

I found the Kabyles in no way annoyed by my painting and
photography, and as usual they had friendly ways, bringing figs
and sour milk when I was at work, and refusing to be paid for
little services. The camera was unluckily knocked down one day
by an eddy of wind, and the falling shutter broken ; a jeweller
soldered it together for me, and refused to accept payment.
Another day, a man brought a good bundle of wood to the tent,
and would take no remuneration ; another offered a couple of
blackbirds as a contribution to my ' pot-au-feu.'

The Kabyles have a reputation for dishonesty, and colonists
have again and again told me, and have most positively in-
sisted that they were all thieves ; but having a limited belief in the
fairness of such warnings, I was always incredulous, and practically
found they deserved a very different character. A solitary instance
of pilfering was all we had to complain of. As we were constantly
surrounded by natives, we might easily have lost more had there
been many ' mauvais sujets' about. I cannot say we were not
tricked sometimes ; what foreigner is not tricked ? But as a rule
I take the Kabyles to be hard bargainers, and afterwards men of
their word ; on more than one occasion I have trusted them,
when they had every opportunity to be dishonest, and I have not
been deceived. They are extremely thrifty, and close with their

money, as most men are who have a hard fight to earn it, and never earn much. I met with a remarkable instance of honesty when staying in the mountains two years ago. Alone, in an out-of-way place, sitting down to make a sketch, I unconsciously dropped my purse. Proceeding perhaps a quarter of a mile, I saw a Kabyle running in hot haste; he overtook me, breathless, but evidently amused about something. I felt much taken aback, when suddenly he handed me my purse. He accepted a present, and I felt most grateful for his honesty, since, though the purse was a light one, it contained every sou that I had in the country, and I by no means regarded it as trash.

On leaving my lodging at Fort National one morning, some faggots were being bought of a poor Kabyle. The transaction was hardly concluded, when a Frenchwoman appearing from a shop next door, said she would take another lot at the same price. The Kabyle replied that on some former occasion she had tried to cheat him, and he would have no dealings with her; he quietly turned his back as he collected his bundles, and then trudged on. She was furious at what she called his insulting language, and called him all the names she could think of. It is a small incident to record, but it is characteristic. Is it credible, for instance, that a Neapolitan could act thus? He would rather esteem a person who had had the wit to overreach him, and scheme till he had cheated in return; he would certainly have been ready with a smooth answer. The story moreover illustrates the principle, that the more people are sinned against, the more they get abused.

The Kabyles are abstemious, tough and wiry; an overfat unwieldy Kabyle is not to be found. Their sobriety, praise be to Mohammed, is absolute ; they drink nothing stronger than coffee. Of course this does not apply to those who live in towns, where they learn to tipple, and I believe become more demoralised, if possible, than the worst class of colonists. It must in honesty be stated, that they are terribly lacking in that virtue which comes next to godliness. That they should not appreciate the luxury of soap and water is the more to be regretted, as it is an inexpensive one. Some of the shepherd lads who came hoping to earn a few coppers by carrying our traps, or by the sale of some trifle, when reproached with uncleanliness, replied, 'I have not another shirt, nor money to buy one.' They pointed out the fragile condition of the one worn, and expressed fear that the rough usage of washing might destroy it altogether. Truly such a situation must be embarrassing, so we said nothing more ; nevertheless, clean shirts became less rare. I am sorry to say that the plague of begging urchins, to be seen wherever tourists go, has already commenced at Fort National. I have never been begged of in the tribes. The needy are given small contributions of food by those who can afford it. Any man, when eating, would as a matter of course and without hesitating, offer a portion to a stranger approaching. The Kabyles are sociable, with unassuming manners. Acquaintances on meeting do not shake hands, but lightly touch them, then raise their fingers to their lips, and kiss them ;[1] then follows a string of expressions, such as, Peace be upon thee, mayest thou abound, good

---

[1] Kissing one's hand is an extremely ancient sign of reverence. It was thus that the sun and moon used to be saluted by their worshippers ; for Job, when he claims integrity in the worship of God, says, ' If my mouth hath kissed my hand : this also were an iniquity to be punished by the judge : f r I should have denied the God that is above.'

be with thee. A chief is saluted with greater deference; he bows
to be kissed in return above the forehead. Compared with Arabs,
Kabyles are industrious; compared with the English, very lazy.
A man will work hard, but likes to do it at his own time; he does
not appreciate the merit of slaving as hard as he can, when engaged
by the day for others. I have watched them at road-making;
as soon as the inspector's back was turned, they would sit down
for a quiet chat, or roll themselves up in their cloaks to take a
nap, or squat and complacently watch a neighbour toil with all
his force at ploughing his own land. I have hardly known
which to admire more, the labourer at the plough, or the phi-
losopher with hands folded in slumber. 'Labor ipse voluptas'
might be the motto of the one; 'Sans gêne' that of the other.

One remarkable feature of Kabylia is the fertility even of the
high ridges. In the tribe of the Beni Ienni there are fields of
wheat and tobacco on the top of the mountain, both crops requir-
ing deep soil. The plough is of the simplest description, and is
carried out to the fields on the shoulder of the ploughman, who
drives a couple of active oxen before him. The yoke is very long
in order to give freedom of action to the beasts when turning on
difficult ground.

The Kabyle begins operations by storing grain in his folded
burnous; this he sows broadcast over the land; he next proceeds
to plough in. The oxen scramble up and down, and in and out,
among silvery-stemmed fig-trees; the driver urging them with a
long rod, and with constant exhortations to work properly, such as,
'Now forwards; keep higher, higher, mind the fig-tree, turn, now
turn, forwards again, oh sons of infidel ones!' Sometimes great

pains are taken with a field, it is ploughed twice or thrice, and all
weeds carefully destroyed. Homer describes ploughing :

> So when two lordly bulls, with equal toil,
> Force the bright ploughshare through the fallow soil,
> Join'd to one yoke the stubborn earth they tear,
> And trace large furrows with the shining share :
> O'er their huge limbs the foam descends in snow
> And streams of sweat down their sour foreheads flow.

A similar picture is given in the ' Georgics.'

> While mountain-snows dissolve against the sun,
> And streams yet new from precipices run,
> Ev'n in this early dawning of the year
> Produce the plough, and yoke the sturdy steer.
> And goad him till he groans beneath his toil,
> Till the bright share is bury'd in the soil.

I give an illustration of this subject. A plough carves its way
slowly through the soil, a crane stands attendant, another flies
free along the valley.

> Mark well the flow'ring almonds in the wood.
> If od'rous blooms the bearing branches load,
> The glebe will to answer the Sylvan reign,
> Great heats will follow, and large crops of grain.

There is a more detailed account of ploughing in the ' Works
and Days' of Hesiod ; it is so faithful a picture in all particulars
of what I have seen in Kabylia, that I cannot refrain from quoting
a few sentences. He mentions the arrival of the cranes from
Africa as a sign for commencing work. In Kabylia they remain
all the winter through.

' Mark too when from on high out of the clouds you shall have
heard the voice of the crane uttering its yearly cry, which both

brings the signal for ploughing and points the season of rainy winter, but gnaws the heart of the man that hath no oxen. Then truly feed the crumpled-horned oxen remaining within their stalls ; for it is easy to say the word, "Lend me a yoke of oxen and a wain," but easy is it to refuse, saying, "There is work for my oxen." But when first the season of ploughing has appeared to mortals, even then rouse thyself. "Pray to the gods," that they may load the ripe holy seed of Demeter, when first beginning thy ploughing, when thou hast taken in hand the goad at the extremity of the plough-tail, and touched the back of the oxen dragging the oaken peg of the pole with the leathern strap. And let the servant boy behind, carrying a mattock, cause trouble to birds whilst he covers over the seed. For good management is best to mortal man, and bad management worst. Thus, if the Olympian god himself after-wards give a prosperous end, will the ears bend to the ground with fulness ; and thou wilt drive the cobwebs from the bins, and I hope that thou wilt rejoice, taking for thyself from substance existing within.'

He concludes by pointing out the right seasons, and says that even a late sower may reap plenteously, if at the first sound of the cuckoo in mid-spring there be three days' steady rain.

In Kabylia I have seen ploughing as late as the middle of April, and followed by much wet, the labour was repaid with a heavy crop.

'But if you shall have ploughed late, this would be your remedy : When the cuckoo sings first on the oak-foliage, and delights mortals over the boundless earth, then let Jove rain three days, and not cease, neither overtopping your ox's hoof-print nor falling short of it ; thus would a late plougher be equal with an early one. But duly observe all things in your mind, nor let either the spring becoming white with blossoms, or the showers returning at set seasons, escape your notice.'

In the valleys there are a great many cranes ; being un-molested, they become very tame, and are often seen following the plough ; the ploughman gives no heed as they stand gravely looking on, or demurely follow his steps.

So the Sicilian reaper sang at work of his love,

> The wolf follows the she-goat, and the crane the plough,
> But I am maddened after thee ;

suggesting that he followed her furious when she fled from him, demurely, and in a state of expectancy for favours to turn up, when she disdainfully suffered his company.

These birds are white, the tips of the wings and tail black, the bill and legs orange. They fly with a flapping motion, and with outstretched necks, like wild duck. It is delightful to watch them settle ; they descend with such a grand self-possessed sweep, suddenly they drop their long yellow legs, and stretch them a little forwards; at that instant they touch the ground, half a second later they are poised and calm, as if they had been standing an hour in meditation. There is sometimes a flock of cranes about a village, where they build on the gourbis or cane-roofed huts. Towards evening they sit in their nests, and make a peculiar rattling noise, by holding the neck back and rapidly clashing the raised bill :

> Like a crane, or a swallow, so did I chatter.

I dined one evening at the house of Salim, the jeweller of the village of Aït l'Arba. He showed me beautiful pieces of old jewellery that he keeps as patterns ; and took me to his workshop, where four or five men were busy. Most of the ornaments which he makes for natives as well as for officers at the Fort, are of small value ; but he is quite capable of making as handsome pieces as of old, if people will give the money. A jeweller of Taourirt Mimoun also showed me large Tafizimen beautifully worked. I never saw such out of the country.

Now that the natives are less well off than they used to be, it can be said of them, as it was of another people of old : ' In that day the Lord will take away the bravery of their tinkling orna-ments about their feet,' ' their round tires like the moon, the chains, and the bracelets, and the mufflers, the bonnets, and the ornaments of the legs, and the headbands, and the tablets, and the ear-rings,' ' the changeable suits of apparel, and the mantles.'

Let us trust that the following verse is not likewise about to become applicable. ' And it shall come to pass, that instead of sweet smell there shall be stink ; and instead of a girdle a rent ; and instead of well-set hair baldness ; and instead of a stomacher a girding of sackcloth ; and burning instead of beauty.' For the pride of the people is cast down, and their spirit broken, and ' in that time shall the present be brought unto the Lord of hosts of a people scattered and peeled, and from a people terrible from their beginning hitherto ; a nation meted out and trodden under foot.'

The blacksmiths at their forges were busy making cutlery. The shape of the knives is always pleasing, and they have sometimes inlaid work. The cheap knives in carved wooden sheaths, that are hawked about Algiers, come from here. In former days, they used also to manufacture guns with long barrels and highly ornamented stocks. These forges are tempting warm nooks in the winter time.

The turning of wooden bowls and dishes is another industry. The piece to be turned is fixed to a chuck revolving backwards and forwards, instead of continually in one direction, as in our lathes. The action is given by a thong lapped round the chuck, attached at one end to a pliable stake fixed in the ground, and at the other, to a treddle worked by the foot of the turner. The action is thus of the same nature as that of a drill worked with a bow.

The women here do not carry their pitchers on their heads, but on their backs. The vases are pointed at the bottom, just like ancient amphoræ. The point rests on the girdle, and the jar is thus steadied, the action of carrying them is not so graceful as the balancing on the head, which always causes a fine carriage.

The women are the only potters, and these amphoræ are made by them in the following manner : A store of clay, cleaned, and properly tempered, is kept at hand in the shade. A rough saucer of clay is first placed on the ground in a sunny spot. On this a woman begins to model a vase ; starting with the solid pointed end, she carries the body up a certain height and leaves it. A second is then begun, and carried to the same point of completion, and so on till half-a-dozen are growing up. Returning to the first, which meanwhile has been drying in the sun, she continues to form the body, bending over, and stepping round and round, with one hand inside she supports the clay as it is added, and with the other smoothes, shapes, and moistens it as required.   The sunlight playing on the wet yellow clay has a pretty effect, and when half formed, the vases have almost the appearance of strange gigantic crocuses.   In spite of the rudeness of the method, the vases come quickly to completion, and are wonderfully true in shape.   The bodies and the spouts with curled-over lips finished, she sits on the ground and models the handles ; before the close of day she will have carried half-a-dozen large amphoræ into the courtyard of her house, where they are left to dry.   As they harden they are rubbed with a smooth piece of wood, laid in the sun, rubbed again, and so on, till they look quite polished.   When in this state I have seen them glisten to such a degree that I was under the impression they were waxed.   In this I was mistaken, for the wife of the Amine of Taourirt el Hadjadj, a good potter, assured me the polish was produced simply by rubbings as described.   The point is interesting, because other wares are found polished instead of glazed.   To complete her work, the potter again sits down, and holding a vessel paints different parts with red ochre, and a variety of patterns drawn in black lines with peroxide of manganese.   A number of vases having been wrought to this state, are put into an open kiln or firepan in the ground, packed with a quantity of wood, which is ignited, and they are thus baked.   Often a final vegetable varnish is passed over them.

Lamps are curiously constructed, consisting of two or three rows of little cups to hold oil one above another ; each cup is connected by a small hole, with an indented projection in front, which serves to hold the wick.   Beneath is a basin to catch the drip, and the whole is supported on a strong round base.

It is singular that the Kabyles, so proficient in moulding vases, dishes, and lamps, and in ornamentation, should yet be unacquainted with such a simple and ancient device as the potter's wheel. This fact points in a very significant manner to the isolation in which they have lived. I have previously described how, in weaving, the woof is passed through the warp with the fingers instead of with a shuttle, a curious proof of the same thing. There is a good collection of Kabyle pottery in the Museum of Native Industries at Algiers, showing great skill, originality, and fancy in the shapes and in the patterns drawn on them.

In Commander Cameron's 'Across Africa,' he describes a woman near Tanganyika Lake making pots, and says that 'the shapes are very graceful and wonderfully truly formed, many being like the amphoræ in the Diomed at Pompeii.'

A vase ending in a point appears at first sight to be an inconvenient arrangement; but it is well adapted to be carried on the back, it cannot be left out in the open, where it is most likely to be exposed to knocks, but must be put away in some corner, when the peg holds it firm.

The fields were now becoming denuded of their crops, and the corn was piled in sheaves on the flat ground about the tent. 'Some on their part indeed were reaping with sharp sickles the staff-like stalks laden with ears, as it were a present of Ceres. Others I wot were binding them in straw ropes, and were laying the threshing floor.'

> While the reaper fills his greedy hands,
> And binds the golden sheaves in brittle bands.

A few days before I left, threshing began. The preparations

surprised me. A party of women brought from the village a large supply of cow-dung, which they mixed with water and spread out. On asking why they made that mess, I was told it was to keep the corn clean. The layer, spread in a large circle, very soon dried hard. The peas (for they began by threshing peas) were heaped upon it, and two yoke of oxen driven over them ; a man followed each yoke, and they circled round and round all the afternoon, till the haulm was broken up, and the peas knocked out.

> Thus with autumnal harvests covered o'er,
> And thick bestrown, lies Ceres' sacred floor,
> When round and round, with never-wearied pain,
> The trampling steers beat out th' unnumbered grain.

When the wind blew freshly, they threw the stuff into the air with wooden pitchforks, and the chaff was winnowed away in clouds.

> And the light chaff, before the breezes borne,
> Ascends in clouds from off the heapy corn,
> The grey dust, rising with collected winds,
> Drives o'er the barn, and whitens all the hinds.

The night after the arrival of my Kabyle servant, he came running into the tent while I supped, to tell me that no less than ten assassins were waiting outside. This news did not upset my appetite, nor was it so alarming as it sounds ; the word assassin being the Kabyle for guard. It was a curious coincidence to be sitting surrounded by 'Assassins,' while the spurs of the mountain facing me were inhabited by the Beni Ismael.

In the Lebanon are tribes known as Assassins. It was the name of a noted fanatical sect of the Ismaelites (one of the great

sections into which Mohammedanism split) formed in the eleventh
century in Persia and Syria. In the latter country their chief
stronghold was in the neighbourhood of Beyrout, and their history
is interwoven with the Crusades.[1] Owing to the objectionable
methods by which they sought to increase their power, their name
was carried by the Crusaders into Europe, and in several modern
languages has become a term expressive of cool premeditated
murder. The origin of the word has been discussed by the
learned, and M. Sylvestre de Sacy narrates a curious story of
Marco Polo's, which has induced him to derive the word from
'Hashishin.' This is the Arabic for 'herbs;' and he endeavours to
prove that the Ismaelites, who committed so many crimes, were
great smokers of Hashish, a well-known intoxicating preparation
of hemp leaves. I leave the etymology of the word to others, but
confess that the theories proposed appear quite fanciful. Moreover the word is far older than the date assigned to it by M.
Sylvestre de Sacy; for it occurs in the Bible in reference to a disturbance in the Holy Land. When St. Paul was arrested in
Jerusalem, on addressing himself to the Roman tribune, the latter
exclaimed, 'Dost thou know Greek? Art thou not then the
Egyptian which before these days stirred up to sedition and led
out into the wilderness the four thousand men of the Assassins?'[2]
Who then were these people? Were they native troops serving
under the Romans, and recruited from hill tribes, answering to our
Sepoys, or to the French Turcos?

---

[1] See Hammer Purgstall, *Geschichte der Assassinen.*

[2] *The Acts,* xxi. 38, revised edition. A correction of 'four thousand men that were
murderers.'

The assassins came regularly, the different villages having been ordered to supply them in rotation, but usually they were only four or five in number. I supplied them with coffee and tobacco, and as they sat round the flickering camp-fire they amused themselves with singing songs which I liked to hear; a succession of plaintive cadences. My impression is, that they were all love-sick assassins, plaintively lamenting to the jealous moon the enforced absence from their loves. Glorious balmy nights they were; the moon shone with splendour, the fields of ripened barley sloped to a mysterious abyss, beyond rose-dim peaks.

> When not a breath disturbs the deep serene,
> And not a cloud o'ercasts the solemn scene;
> Around her throne the vivid planets roll,
> And stars unnumbered gild the glowing pole,
> O'er the dark trees a yellower verdure shed
> And tip with silver every mountain's head.

There are professional minstrels in Kabylia who repeat songs, tales, and sayings handed down by tradition, and who also invent new ones. They wander about the country after the harvests of corn, figs, and olives, and are paid not in money, but in kind. In some tribes the minstrel receives an annual gift, which can be considered as a pension provided from the communal purse. Some who have the gift of invention stop at home, but their compositions are sung through the country, nevertheless; for itinerant minstrels come from afar to learn, and thus make additions to their stock. The musician warbles running cadences on a reed-pipe, sings a verse, and warbles on the pipe again; he will thus continue tuneful for a whole afternoon, halting occasionally to chat a while with his audience. A number of such songs have been collected by General A. Hanoteau. Many refer to engagements with the French at the time of the conquest, others are of a more general character. I translate a few as samples.

The first verse of the following song is a picture of war; the second, of stormy weather. These introduce the motive of the third; ordinary means of communication being interrupted, a lover entreats a bird to carry a message to his mistress. In the verses that follow, he gives an account of how he fell into his present love sick condition, and represents the lady as returning his affection. It will be remarked that in these latter verses there is an echo of the two that are introductory. A picture is given of domestic insubordination to legitimate authority, and attachment to the free lover; the path of true love is beset with uncertainty and storms, the road to domestic happiness is blocked. The Kabyle law must be kept in mind, that a man can, when he wishes, repudiate his wife, and that she cannot marry again without he approves of the new aspirant to her hand.

SONG.

I.

The Bey has raised the banner of war;
In his honour the flag is flying.
He leads warriors gaily apparelled
With spurs well adjusted on their boots.
Those hostile to them, they with shouts destroy;
They have brought the rebels to their senses.

II.

Snow falls heavily.
Thick mist precedes the lightning.
Branches bend to the ground.
The highest trees are split.
The shepherd cannot pasture his flock.
The roads to the markets are closed.

III.

Kind, friendly falcon,
Spread thy wings, fly.
If thou art a friend, favour me.
Dawn precedes sunrise.
Fly to her house ; rest there.
Perch upon the sill of the gracious beauty.

IV.

Speak to the gazelle of thyme-covered plains,
To the beauty of radiant freshness,
To the mistress of the odorous necklace.
When she passes, the street appears festive.
Would she were my bride !   We should find peace ;
Otherwise, we shall be drowned in sin.

V.

She said, ' I condemn thee not, oh noble one !
I am steadfast to my sworn word.
I am in the hands of a wicked man.
He refuses to divorce me.
We are both of us in torments.
Thou and I can no longer be parted.'

VI.

In what manner did I lose my senses ?
I saw her through the chink of her door.
Tears streamed from her eyes,
Like a river when it floods its banks.
For her I would sacrifice my life.
What deeds can the wicked dare ?

VII.

I am like unto a poet.
For my well-beloved only among rebels
I improvise a new song.
Her love has fastened upon me; I burn with desire.
O cheikh, grant her her liberty !
She is put on one side, without power to remarry.

PROVERBS.

He who is slothful is foolish at heart ;
He is badly prompted.   The cares of this world are enduring.

Love him who loves thee ; avoid him who hates thee.
He whom everyone esteems an evil-doer
Cannot be of use to thee ; seek him not.
Thus says tradition.   The law even punishes with death.

He who grafts upon an oleander performs a vain act ;
He is wanting in sense.   Thus to make friends with a nigger
Is to act like one who eats carrion.

Whoso cannot fight, let him be patient, that is best.
A man of sense watches over himself.
The fool waits till he be covered with shame before he opens his eyes.

The cure for cold is fire ; there is nothing like it in winter.
In summer let it alone, until there be reason to draw near it.

The best quality is politeness.   Gravity adds to consideration.
Thoughtlessness is insipid.   Boasting is a false pride.

Treason comes from friends or from allies.
The enemy has no means to hurt thee.
Thus says K'hala.   Understand thou of unsullied blood.

If honey flowed like a river, if women were to be found like locusts, if there were no masters, men would be cloyed with marriage.   New mistresses would come and go.

When a woman is cross-grained, reckon that her lord does not please her.   She does nothing becomingly.   Her tongue is always ready to attack.   Her husband will be covered with confusion, like a house that has a vicious dog.

Let him who marries take a woman of good birth, a girl noble and chaste.   A bad marriage is like the setting of the sun, darkness follows quickly upon it.

Honour to him who pulls the trigger, who scales the heights.   He has banished fear from his heart.   Thus says K'hala.   The protection of the Prophet be upon him until death.

A ROUND.

I.

Thou, oh Lord, who hast caused the fruits of autumn to ripen !
Grant me Tasadith with the graceful garments.

II.

Thou, oh Lord, who hast created pomegranates !
Grant me Fatima with the dark eyelashes.

III.

Thou, oh Lord, who hast created apples !
Prompt Yamina to say to me ' Come.'

IV.

Thou, oh Lord, who hast created pears !
Grant me El-Yasmin with the arched eyebrows !

V.

Thou, oh Lord, who hast created quinces !
Grant me Dehabia.   May she become a widow !

VI.

Thou, oh Lord, who hast created the young figs !
Grant me Aïni.   May the old fellow perish !

VII.

Thou, oh Lord, who hast ordained unequal lots !
Thou hast given to some, and the others are jealous.

VIII.

Thou, oh Lord, who hast given us extra good things !
Grant me Adidi.   Keep far from us the Angel of Death.

INCENTIVE TO WORK.

I.

We will swear to it if thou wilt,
By the mosques of Ibahalal.
Thy husband wants to remarry.
He will wed one like the full moon.
He will take care of her at home.
As for thee, thou wilt look after the donkeys.
Lift thy feet,
Frisk about.

II.

We will swear to it, if thou wilt,
By Sidi Aïsh.
Thy husband wants to marry.
He will wed one who will give him a son,
He will take care of her at home.
As for thee, thou wilt gather herbs.
> Lift thy feet,
> Frisk about.

III.

We will swear to it, if thou wilt,
By the mosque of Aït Boubedir.
Thy husband wants to remarry.
He will wed one decked with jewels.
He will take care of her at home.
As for thee, thou wilt work at the wool.
> Lift thy feet,
> Frisk about.

IV.

We will swear to it, if thou wilt,
By the mosques of Sheurfa.
Thy husband wants to remarry.
He will wed Tharifa.
She for his bed,
Thou for the fields.
> Lift thy feet,
> Frisk about.

VERSES ON MARRIAGE.

I.

To choose a wife in one's village
Is to shave off the beard.
She will make uphill work,
And thou wilt yet have to descend.

II.

A wrinkled woman
Scares away luck.
Even the rats, on her approach,
Scamper out of the village.

III.

Beware of marriage with a lean woman ;
Be towards her as a woman put away who cannot remarry.
Take only a young girl ;
She it is who will suit thee.

IV.

A woman neither fat nor thin
Is like a wood with flowers.
When she is cheerful,
Everything is bright to thee.

V.

Beware of marriage with one put away,[1]
She is like a sack of prickly brushwood.
Everyday there will be disputes
To trouble the neighbours.

[1] See the advice Hesiod gives to his brother, 'an habitual loafer.' 'First of all get a house, and a woman, and a ploughing ox. A woman purchased, not wedded.' I read

VI.

A silly babbler is like a spent ball.
If thou measurest an arm
She adds a span to the length.

VII.

To marry a woman with a projecting forehead
Is a cause for mourning.
By Allah! I would not have her,
No, not for sheepskin.

VIII.

To marry a proud woman
Is a matter for shame.
By Allah! I would not have her,
No, not for the sole of my shoe.

IX.

To marry a cousin
Is sour to my soul.
I pray Thee, O God!
Preserve me from this misfortune.

X.

To marry a niece,
By God! I refuse to do it.
In this, my heart is the master
Which dictates the lesson.

that Aristotle evidently believes that wife is here understood, and hence some think that the second line is spurious. Does not the difficulty arise from looking at it from a modern European standpoint? The whole passage is perfectly applicable to Kabyle society. More advice follows : ' Most of all marry her who lives near you, when you have duly looked round on everything, lest you should marry a cause-of-mocking for your neighbours.' I conclude that the advice of the song not to marry in one's village, is in order to avoid bickerings and interference from relatives, leading to loss of dignity, like shaving off the beard. Better to be on the safe side, and seek for a girl unknown to the neighbourhood, who, separated from friends, will not bring upon you causes for mocking.

XI.

Let a man take a woman that is well born.
Birth guarantees good manners.
The sick heart is restored,
And rejoices in the pleasures of this world.

A WOMAN'S REPLY.

Go child! It is useless to beat water in order to make butter. Thou art old, and I have not yet commenced to fast during Ramadan. Thy head is grey, thy legs are feeble, thou hast lost thy wits, and talkest not of present things. That which remaineth for thee here is a tomb. As for me, I will marry him who pleaseth me.

A WOMAN'S WAR-SONG.

He who wishes to possess women, flinches not on the day of combat. He conducts himself bravely when the bullets whistle. He shall choose among the young girls. Oh, dear name of Amelkher!

TALE.

An old man had seven sons. His wife died, and he remained a widower. One day his sons were seated and talking. The youngest of them said to his brothers, ' Come, O my brothers! let us sell some goats, and with the price of them marry our father again.' They dropped this subject of conversation, and passed on to another.

The old man said to them, ' Let us return to the conversation about the goats.'

The weather grew very hot, though not oppressive, for a fresh breeze sprang up in the middle of the day, and blew till four or five o'clock, a blast most grateful to perspiring mortals, but sometimes accompanied with eddies of wind, which the natives called thaboushithant.

The children, when they saw an eddy approach, would leave off
their play of building villages, that is, piling stones into little heaps,
with bits of stick placed upright atop to represent mosque towers,
and for fun run in its way, when their burnouses, caught up and
twisted, flying about their heads, would wrap them in confusion.
Thus do the children indulge in the building of imagined houses,
vain castle-building, for

> The sportive wanton, pleased with some new play,
> Sweeps the slight works and fashion'd domes away.

In spite of this grateful breeze, I was glad to keep quiet in
the middle of the day.   How impressive is the hour of noon in the
south !   When the sun rides in triumphant power overhead, and
showers his fervid rays upon the earth, and the sky has lost its
deep blue, and is of a palpitating grey, towards the horizon quite
warm and glowing ; when the trees twinkle with innumerable
stars of light, and distant rocky crags glitter through the purple
bloom of distance ; when cattle seek the shade, and the harvester
puts aside his sickle, for 'reapers ought to begin at the rising of
the crested lark, and to cease when it goes to rest ; but to keep
holiday during the heat.'   Insect life alone is quickened, and the
air is all athrob with heat, and the loud incessant songs of the
cicala.

Then it is that the mountains are most beautiful, though there
is a fascination about them under all aspects, and whatever their
mood.

At dawn ; when the light of the rising sun touching them,
breaks their massed shadows with a joyous greeting.

In the evening ; when they blush and glow at his departure.

Through the fresh clearness of a spring day ; when robed in blue, they look majestically serene.

In a spring morning ; when they are half veiled by rising mists which by-and-by will be gently driven in flocks of clouds across the azure meads of heaven.

During the calm mellow afternoon; when the contented land basks in sunshine at their feet, and their summits are capped with fantastic battlements of cloud.

During the ominous lull preceding a sirocco, the air thick and yellow, when they become mysterious and ghostly, hooded with pallid white.

In the thunderstorm, when they are of deepest purple, to be engulfed in the black clouds, from which dart forked lightnings ; for offended Jove

> his glory shrouds
> Involv'd in tempests, and a night of clouds,
> And from the middle darkness flashes out,
> By fits he deals his fiery bolts about.

Sometimes I have stood on a height in the tumult of a storm, in the whirl of driving mists, when a rent was suddenly torn in the black canopy, and for an instant, the lofty crags were seen glistening against the deep sky, calm, like sustaining hope in the time of trouble. Sometimes, rejoicing in the freshness of a glorious winter's morning, I have fancied, that upon their lustrous summits is spread a carpet for the immortals, for

> Not proud Olympus yields a nobler sight,
> Tho' Gods assembled grace his tow'ring height,
> Than what more humble mountains offer here,
> Where, in their blessings, all those Gods appear.

At noon, while ' the tuneful cicala, perched on a tree, poured forth a shrill song from under his wings,' I used to spread a cloth in the shade, and ' with face turned to catch the brisk-blowing Zephyr,' reclined there rejoicing.   Mohammed sat by my side, and devised new patterns to be carved upon my stick of wild olive. My neighbour of the threshing-floor, with a wreath of pea wound round his head, the curling tendrils falling on his shoulders, squatted hard by, contemplating the heaped-up corn, whilst he pictured capacious bins overflowing with a bountiful store.

The pipe in my mouth was not a melodious one, but there rose from it a fragrant cloud—as I may say—an incense, grateful I trust, to her who has ever been honoured in these regions ; ' the mountain nymph, sweet Liberty.'

In these uplands during the noontide lull, or at tranquil evening, does she not revisit her haunts, and bless the careworn husbandman ?

> O happy, if he knew his happy state !
> The swain, who, free from business and debate.
> Receives his easy food from Nature's hand,
> And just returns of cultivated land.

But the time had arrived to retreat from sylvan bowers and return to the more civilised homes of men.

On June 24 I struck the tent ; while the shades of night yet slumbered upon the mountains, and the people began descending to renew their labours.   ' Make you haste ; gather and bring home your corn, rising at the dawn, that you may have substance sufficient.   For the morning obtains by lot a third share of the day's work.   The morn, look you, furthers a man on his road, and furthers him too in his work ; the morn, I say, which at its appearing sets many men on their road, and places the yoke on many oxen.'

AMONG THE TOMBS.

As when ashore an infant stands,
And draws imagin'd houses in the sands.

POPE'S *Iliad*, Book xv.

After seeing my effects packed on mules, I sent off Mohammed with them to Tizi Ouzou, starting myself for the Fort, where I had matters to arrange.

I had never before seen the place in its summer dress, and was surprised at the transformation ; for its ugly little houses were half hidden in verdure, and the acacias lining the road were of an astonishingly rich green.

At the inn I learned that Dominique had remained two or three days, making such amends as he could for his long abstinence from liquor. There also I met some of the Fathers, with whom I dined ; and having done my business, and bid good-bye to Madame Pierre, who had in many ways been most attentive, I took omnibus to Tizi Ouzou.

I found my luggage in a pile, and faithful Mohammed sitting on the top keeping guard. We parted on the best of terms.

The following morning I arrived at Algiers. Muirhead, who had already returned from his trip to Constantine, tried to induce me to return by sea ; but I was proof against the attractions of the swell in the Bay of Biscay, and instead, took the overland journey by Marseilles.

A few days later, I was back in the Great City, where the sun cares not much to show his face, and the heavens seem to be ever weeping over the sins of the people.

Spottiswoode & Co., Printers, New-street Square, London.